HOMICIDE: Life on the Street

HOMICIDE:

WHITE BUTTERFLIES

JEROME PREISLER

BERKLEY BOULEVARD BOOKS, NEW YORK

HOMICIDE: WHITE BUTTERFLIES

A Berkley Boulevard Book / published by arrangement with National Broadcasting Company, Inc.

PRINTING HISTORY
Berkley Boulevard edition / May 1998

The Penguin Putnam Inc. World Wide Web site address is
http://www.penguinputnam.com

ISBN: 0-425-16494-2

BERKLEY BOULEVARD
Berkley Boulevard Books are published by The Berkley Publishing Group,
a member of Penguin Putnam Inc.,
200 Madison Avenue, New York, New York 10016.
BERKLEY BOULEVARD and its logo are trademarks
belonging to Berkley Publishing Corporation.

PRINTED IN THE UNITED STATES OF AMERICA

10   9   8   7   6   5   4   3   2   1

For our dog, Joney, whose seventeen years were far too short. We love you with all our hearts, sweet girl, and will remember you as long as memory remains.

How dreadful knowledge of the truth can be
when there's no help in truth!
—Sophocles, *Oedipus Rex*

ONE

EVERY NOW AND then she fantasized about walking away from it all, maybe opening a gift shop in Ocean City, where she'd spend half the year selling beach towels, Day-Glo rubber crabs, and lacquered seashells to tourists. Live the other six months in Florida—say, someplace like Naples or Sanibel—watching Max cavort in the sand and torment the gulls and pelicans. She'd heard there were plenty of younger people in those towns, people her own age who'd had enough of the hustle and chase. And maybe she'd find romance there . . . really, why not? Drift off into the sunset with Mr. Right on a seventy-foot yacht there in Florida.

So, okay, that was *only* a fantasy, she thought, waiting for the cashier at the gourmet shop to pack the dinner she was bringing home, a couple of roll-up sandwiches filled with fresh mozzarella, basil, and arugula, *bon appétit*. As her first boss had told her years ago, the trade was the thing. And she still burned for it, burned for it deep inside, never mind that she often felt as if she were being held together by a very thin thread. Despite what it could do to you on a personal level, how it could eat you up, it was a powerful addiction.

Now she took her bag from the cashier, said good night, and pushed out the door into the chill evening air. At six-thirty, it was already dark, not to mention overcast and damp. Where had summer gone? Though the calendar said it was the twenty-eighth of October, and daylight saving time had ended earlier in the week, she didn't feel ready for this kind of weather.

Well, at least the rain had been holding off, and would hopefully continue doing so until she got home. She had left her umbrella in the closet, ignoring the storm forecasts, thinking it would be a pain to carry it around while walking the dog and picking up dinner from the store. Still, she ought to have learned by now that God had invented totes for a reason. Getting drenched would be the perfect clincher for an already perfectly miserable day.

Over near the curb, Max was barking to show his displeasure at having been left behind on the street, and she hurried to untie his leash from the parking meter she'd looped it around before entering the store. After prancing around her legs a bit, the shih tzu began pulling toward home, clearly feeling a lot more energetic than she did at the moment.

It was worth noting, however, that Max did nothing but sleep all afternoon, curled on his little doggie cushion, while she was out roughing it up in the world—a *man's* world, let us remember—fighting to stay on top of the game.

She walked on down the block, Max tugging at her arm, her coat flapping around her legs. Sanibel, Naples, Boca, warm sunlit days and cool starlit nights . . . the truth was, it would all bore the hell out of her before too long. Competition both drew and drove her, and it had been that way as far back as she could remember. Even before high school and college, before the athletics trophies and academic honors, she had placed heavy demands on herself, and nothing had changed when she'd made her choice of professions. What was it one of the Great Wallendas had said? *Life begins and ends on the wire.* It was like that for her. Definitely like that. Starting out every day knowing that multi-million-dollar commissions, and in some cases whole corporate futures, were balancing on how well she performed. The stresses were enormous. Constant. Especially since she'd launched the new division. She had thought she was being realistic about that, and had known she would have to make her share of sacrifices. But until lately the rewards, the *success,* had made the price seem almost insignificant. It had taken a great deal of turmoil for her to see the real cost of what she'd achieved . . . and the episode she'd had with Durham earlier that day only proved she still had a lot to learn.

In hindsight, she supposed her biggest mistake all along had been believing there were parts of her life that could be kept out of the arena.

Reaching the corner now, she waited for the light to change, crossed the street with a handful of second-wave rush hour commuters and continued for another half block before pausing in front the local greengrocer's. She stood there a moment, debating whether to pick up a few pieces of fruit—an orange or grapefruit for breakfast, maybe some bananas to snack on while she watched Leno. But Max was being a nag, tugging at the leash to let her know he wanted to get home, and she decided not to quarrel with him.

She turned from the produce bins in front of the store and strode toward home, barely aware of the homeless guy coming toward her on the sidewalk, his head bent against the rising wind. In fact, she might not have noticed him at all if it hadn't been for her dog suddenly starting to growl as he approached. Donna might have found this behavior unusual, except that Max was already skittish from having been leashed to the meter, and had a habit of continuing to make a nuisance of himself once he got going.

"*Shhhh,* c'mon, that's enough!" she said, glancing briefly at the derelict as she yanked back on the leash, thinking it probably wasn't such a bad thing the pooch was making a racket. She'd seen this guy hanging around the area before, or thought she had, at least—some of these people, they became neighborhood fixtures for a while and then just kind of disappeared. Or sometimes they turned up in a different part of town, begging for change on virgin turf, where the usual run of passersby hadn't gotten tired of the pitch.

Anyway, the guy was hardly a model of cleanliness and she really didn't want him getting too close.

Huddled into a threadbare army coat, his long black hair spilling from under his watch cap in a greasy tangle, he came abreast of her, still heading in the opposite direction, moving along at a fairly good pace. His hands were in his pockets as he passed.

Still barking, Max had abruptly stopped on the sidewalk and was snapping at the air as if he'd gotten tired of being a shih tzu, and had decided to start behaving like a pit bull instead. This was not just unusual, this was downright *weird*. She could remember him acting up like this only once before, but that had been under very different circumstances.

"Max, be *quiet*," she said. The homeless man was behind her now, and Max was getting his leash fouled around her ankles as he actually spun in a circle, still barking and snapping at the guy.

Sighing with aggravation, she bent over to untangle the leash, and had nearly extricated herself when the homeless man unexpectedly whirled on her, stepping close, his left hand coming out of his coat pocket, his left hand holding a gun . . .

Dear God, she thought . . .

He was pulling a *gun* out of his pocket.

Her heart jolting in her chest, she straightened and looked at him, her eyes filling with horror and disbelief.

"No, please—" she said, and then he took another step toward her and squeezed the trigger, the gun going off less than six inches from where she stood with her dog yapping away like crazy and its leash wrapped around her legs.

She staggered backward, feeling the bullet slam into her chest, that look of terrified surprise still stamped on her features. Staggered back, tripping over the leash, and had just enough time to see the blood flowering brightly over the front of her raincoat when a second slug blasted from the gunbarrel, caught her in the left side of her stomach and knocked her off her feet. She sprawled on the pavement, her body on fire, a slippery wetness leaking out of her, soaking through her clothes. Somewhere around her she heard people's voices, and Max barking, and she struggled to raise herself onto her elbows, and then saw the bore of the gun angle downward, lowering to her face, and a third, fourth and fifth round were fired in rapid succession, fired at her head at point-blank range, the explosions driving her scream back into her throat and instantly ending her life out there on the sidewalk.

A split second later the killer ran off, racing down the block, turning the corner, fleeing from the crowd of stunned eyewitnesses that had begun to gather around his victim as the dog kept barking and barking and barking into the chill autumn night. . . .

TWO

EVERYBODY ON THE shift pretty much thought Tim Bayliss was strange.

Well, maybe that was putting it too strongly.

Unusual, then.

No, too mild.

Unconventional? Eccentric?

"Not quite," Detective John Munch said to the other men in the coffee room, going on to explain that both words implied an untroubled freedom from conformity, a casual, even careless disregard of the norm. Whereas Bayliss always seemed to be seeking approval from his fellows in the homicide unit.

Which left . . . what? Weird? Quirky? Flaky?

"You ask me," Meldrick Lewis said, "Timmy's *buggin'*."

"A verb doesn't really fit in this instance," Munch said.

"A what?" Lewis said, taking a bite of his roll.

"Jesus, don't you remember your elementary school grammar? A verb expresses an *action*."

"Such as the words strangle, shoot, and stab," Frank Pembleton said. "Off the top of my head."

"Exactly." Munch poured some coffee for himself. "You see, saying Timmy's *bugging* would mean he's in the process of entering a certain state of being, rather than already *in* that state. Which rules out that particular term. What we've gotta stick with here are *adjectives.*"

"For example, words like—"

"That's all right, I get the idea," Lewis grumbled. "Appreciate you fellas takin' me to the next level."

"You ask me, I think 'odd' kinda fits."

This from J. H. Brodie, the only man present who was not a detective or, for that matter, a duly appointed officer of the Baltimore Police Department, but rather a videographer employed by the BCPD's crime scene unit. Looking like one of the Bowery Boys in a too large suit and gray fedora with an upturned brim, he shouldered his camera and aimed it into the squad room, where Bayliss had cornered Mike Kellerman at his desk.

"Know what I think, Brodie?" Lewis said.

"What?" Brodie peered into the viewer and thumbed the Record button.

"I think the oddest bird around here is you."

"Let's not digress, gentlemen," Munch said. "Tonight's subject of discussion is Timmy."

"Is this game just for the boys, or can anybody play?" Sgt. Kay Howard asked, shuffling past Brodie into the coffee room, her long red hair tumbling over her shoulders like dawnlight over the bonny hills and dales of her ancestral Ireland.

"This group finds any form of exclusion intolerable, and it especially abhors sexism," Munch said. "*Most* especially since you outrank the rest of us."

Howard slipped a bag of herbal tea from its wrapper, dropped it into a cup of hot water, and left it to steep on the counter beside the electric burner.

"All right, here's the word," she said, and then paused momentarily for effect, forming quotation marks with her fingers. "*Juvenile.*"

The rest of them looked at each other in silence . . . all except Brodie, who had kept his camcorder on Bayliss and Kellerman.

"Uh-uh," Lewis said finally. "Don't fit him in the least."

"Absolutely not," Munch said. "Right, Frank?"

Pembleton shrugged and rose from where he'd been sitting at the table.

"I've got work to do," he said, and left the room.

Howard looked puzzled.

"What's eating him?"

"Your casting aspersions on Bayliss's manhood, is what," Munch said.

"Cold," Lewis muttered under his breath, "real cold."

"But you guys were just talking about Tim being *nuts.*"

Munch and Lewis shook their heads.

"You hear any of us use that word, Munch?"

"Nope. Can't even imagine it."

"Me neither."

"We better move on."

They walked out the door, still shaking their heads.

Howard sighed, went back over to the counter, and reached for her steaming mug.

"Jesus, Brodie," she said, turning toward him. "You'd think I'd said Tim was some kind of—"

She cut herself off in midsentence.

Brodie had already followed the others into the squad room, his camera humming away on his shoulder.

Leaving her quite alone.

"Juvenile assholes," she said to the four walls.

Standing at Kellerman's desk, a pack of Aviator playing cards in his hands, Bayliss watched the other detectives file into the room and grinned with delight. He'd been wondering what the hell was taking them so long in the coffee room this morning, his newly learned card trick—well, feat of legerdemain, to stick with the term that was used in the book he'd been studying for the past month—his premier demonstration of legerdemainic skill being a ridiculous waste of time without an audience.

"Come one, come all," he announced. "My dear friends, let me have your attention. I hope you're prepared to be mystified and astonished, struck *speechless,* in fact, by a spectacle unlike any you've seen before—"

"Ain't no *question* he's making a spectacle of himself," Lewis whispered to Munch.

"I'm left agog by his idiocy," Munch replied.

"Can we please get this over with?" Pembleton said.

"Okay, okay, it'll just take five minutes," Bayliss said irritably, wondering why he'd thought these drips would get caught up in the fun spirit of his exhibition in the first place. "Now listen close, because there's a story that goes with this trick. . . . It's called, uh, the Three Scuzzball Perps, by the way."

He riffled the cards. Actually, the trick was called the Four Scurvy Knaves—but the magic book he'd picked up for a dime at a Salvation Army sidewalk sale had been printed in England around 1910, and he figured some updating was badly needed.

"All right, the first thing I want is for one of you skeptics to cut the deck," he said.

"Who says we're skeptical?" Kellerman said.

"You're cops, aren't you?"

"He's got a point there," Pembleton said, and reached out to oblige Bayliss.

"Next," Bayliss said, "I'd like somebody to remove the jacks from the pack, then hand them back to me."

Lewis scowled. "Yo, Tim, wassup with you? I mean, we got open cases to investigate—"

"I told you it'll only take five minutes," Bayliss said. "If you guys quit interrupting me."

The frown on Lewis's face deepened.

"Gimme the cards," he said, grabbing them from Pembleton and fishing out the jacks.

"All right, we're in business." Bayliss took the cards

back from him, keeping the slim pile of jacks separate and putting the rest of the pack down on Kellerman's desk blotter. "Here's the story. There are these four perps . . . that's the jacks, see . . ."

"Surprise, surprise," Munch said.

". . . and they're pretty inexperienced. A bunch of up-and-comers out to make their rep with a big score. So they decide to rip off an apartment building, which is represented by the *deck*—"

"Clever," Pembleton said, checking his watch.

Bayliss glared at him.

"As I was saying," he said, holding up the jack of clubs, "they hit an apartment building, and this creep right here in my hand—his handle's Club, okay?—Club breaks in through the basement."

He placed the card on the bottom of the deck and then displayed the jack of spades.

"Now this guy, name of Spade—"

"I'll try not to take offense," Pembleton said.

"Me neither," Lewis said.

"Spade goes straight to the roof," Bayliss continued, ignoring them.

"Why's that?" Munch said.

Bayliss shrugged. "I dunno, what's the difference?"

"Maybe he knows the door up there doesn't have a lock," Kellerman offered. "Either that or he's planning to climb down the fire escape into somebody's window."

"But his boy Club already got in through the basement," Lewis said. "Why don't he just follow *him?*"

12

"The window's the better choice if he's targeting a specific apartment," Pembleton said. "Save him the trouble of having to get through the front door, which for all we know has *multiple* locks, and could be wired to a burglar alarm—"

"Look, it isn't important," Bayliss said. "These are street guys, *users,* meaning their heads aren't screwed on straight, so who can figure?" He put the jack of spades on top of the deck, then cut the deck a second time. "As you can see, we are now left with two members of the crew—"

"Heart and Diamond," Munch said.

"Right, those are their names, but I really wish you'd leave the patter to me," Bayliss snapped. He took a deep breath. "Anyway, Heart and Diamond are brothers, and both of them are kind of uptight about this score, being it's the first one they've ever been on. So uptight that neither of them wants to go up on the roof *or* down to the basement, what you'd consider the vulnerable extremities of the house."

"You mind runnin' that by me again?" Lewis said.

"Could be they're phobic," Munch said.

"That's exactly what they are: phobic. These are two phobic and cowardly thieves," Bayliss said. "Well, here they are—and I want all of you to *picture* this, 'cause it's pretty funny—here they are, shaking and sweating, clinging to each other's shirtsleeves, *bawling,* even. A couple of pathetic screwups who never should've gotten involved in this job to start with—"

"Time's a-wasting," Pembleton said, glancing at his watch again.

"Relax, I'm almost done," Bayliss said. "Now, where was I?"

"Tellin' us about the Chickenshit brothers," Lewis said.

"Yeah, thanks. Well, these two weepy-eyed losers go to the middle of the house, okay? . . ." Bayliss waved the cards in the air, laid them atop one of the two piles on the desk, then put the second half of the deck on top of it. "Are you guys really visualizing this? I mean, nobody's laughing. . . ."

"How much longer do you figure this will take?" Pembleton said.

Bayliss looked at him and picked up the full pack of cards.

"It's over, Frank," he said angrily, still glaring at him as he split the pack in two again and pulled all four jacks out of the middle. "As you can see, the whole crew wound up gathering in the center of the house, though everybody saw me put them in different places."

"That's it, huh?" Lewis said.

"Yeah," Bayliss said. "The end."

"Shoulda figured this was gonna be a waste of time."

"Hey, what exactly did you expect?"

"A *trick,* for one thing."

"What do you call it when all four cards turn up in the *middle*—"

"C'mon, man, get real. The whole thing just didn't work."

"Yeah?" Bayliss said. "Why's that?"

"'Cause it's obvious, is why," Lewis said.

"Obvious?"

"An' dull."

Bayliss looked around at the others. "The rest of you agree?"

They nodded in silent unison.

Fuming, he tapped the pack of cards on the desk to even out its edges, then slipped it into his pants pocket.

"Calm down, Timmy-boy," Munch said. "So, big deal, the card trick stank—"

"It wouldn't have stunk if you guys hadn't kept rushing me."

"Oh?" Munch said. "FYI, it was your partner Frank who couldn't take his boredom-glazed eyes off his watch."

"And *you* were the one who started with the *phobic* nonsense—"

"Excuse me, fellows."

Upon hearing the deep, low rumble of his voice, the five detectives looked over at Lieutenant Al Giardello, who had come padding out of his office at one end of the squad room, a case report in his hand. A tall, broad-shouldered black man who had inherited virtually none of his Sicilian father's features but all of his fondness for homemade pasta and bel canto opera, Giardello had an unsettling habit of sneaking up on you in the high-topped Keds that were his constant, unaccountable deviation from the otherwise crisp formality of his attire.

"Shame as it is to divert anyone from this stimulating conversation, I'm obliged to inform you that a murder squeal has just come in," he said.

"Do as you must, O Chief," Pembleton said.

"Thank you." Giardello smiled and handed him the sheet of paper he'd carried out of his office. "And just to show how much I appreciate your understanding, I'm sending you and Bayliss out on this case."

"We're honored." Pembleton's face became serious as he scanned the report. "Doesn't tell us much. The victim's a woman, shot repeatedly on the sidewalk on Howard Street."

"That's Fell's Point," Bayliss said, mildly surprised. "Usually a quiet part of town."

"Not tonight," Giardello said. "We've got some uniforms at the scene, but they have their hands full with gawkers, and I want you taking charge before any evidence gets stepped on."

"It should only take us five, ten minutes to drive there," Pembleton said.

"Why doesn't Bayliss the Great wave a magic wand over your heads and utter a spell of teleportation?" Munch said. "Be even faster that way."

"Very funny, Munch," Giardello said, jabbing a finger at him. "Since you're so quick with the helpful suggestions, I'd like you to go with them."

"Gee, I've got to finish my paperwork on the Jackson case—"

"Work on it later," Giardello said. "Now get moving."

He stood there a moment, smiling broadly, and then turned and glided back toward his office.

"Presto, I'm screwed," Munch said, and went to put on his topcoat.

It got so there was a numbing sameness to every murder scene. The zippered body bags, the morgue wagons, the uniformed officers, the squad cars and flashing lights, the hivelike activity of the evidence technicians, the bystanders pressing against the boundaries marked off by the yellow police tape.

It got so your stomach no longer turned to ash at the sight of a woman sprawled on the pavement with half her head gone, her bloodstained coat pulled up and twisted around her body, her skirt bunched around her waist, and her legs : . .

They were long, slender, attractive legs, the legs of someone who had kept in shape, who had taken very good care of herself. . . .

"Has anybody made an ID?" Pembleton asked, shouldering through the crowd of looky-loos and ducking under the tape to approach the victim.

The patrolmen who'd responded to the 911 told him no one had.

Pembleton stood there gazing down at her, a woman lying dead on the pavement, her clothes sodden and covered with blood, her legs—it almost embarrassed him to have noticed their loveliness—spread in a position of final, conspicuous indignity. She had been shot in the face more than once, and her remaining eye was staring insipidly up into the rain that was falling from the sky, mixing with her blood as it streamed over the wet asphalt and guttered down the curb. . . .

"What about the medical examiner? She finished with her yet?"

The patrolmen both shrugged uncertainly.

Pembleton wondered whether these two had any inkling of what they were supposed to be doing here.

He kept looking down at her.

A woman lying dead and exposed on the sidewalk in the driving rain.

The detectives had recorded their time of arrival as 1925 hours, or 7:25 P.M., carefully noting that the victim *appeared* dead rather than flatly stating she *was* dead, a fact that was immediately obvious to all of them, as well as anybody else on the street who wasn't blind. This was called going strictly by the book, and it was what every conscientious investigator had been doing ever since a bunch of slimebag West Coast defense lawyers—well, actually, there were almost as many East Coast lawyers on their scheme-team—had gotten a guilty-as-hell celebrity client acquitted on a double murder rap, partially because of sloppy police procedures.

"Nineteen twenty-five hours, rainy and dark. Victim female, white, approximately five foot six, mid-thirties. Blond hair, shoulder length. Wearing a gray jacket, light blue blouse, black skirt, black stockings, black shoes. Appears dead," Pembleton said, speaking into his minicassette recorder.

By the book.

He clicked off the tape recorder and turned to Bayliss.

"Do we have eyewitnesses?"

"Maybe a half dozen. The shooter didn't seem too worried about people on the street getting a look at him."

"Make sure they stay put." Pembleton gestured toward the paw prints on the bloody ground. "Where's the dog?"

"We stuck it in the backseat of our car," the younger of the two uniforms said. "Didn't know what else to do with it."

"Damn thing just keeps barking like crazy," the older cop said.

"I'll want to see it in a few minutes. Meanwhile, try to get it to drink some water. It's easy for dogs to become dehydrated when they're under stress."

"This neighborhood, maybe I should buy it some Evian," the older cop muttered.

"What was that?"

"Nothing, nothing."

Pembleton watched them walk off toward their cruiser, then turned toward Bayliss and Munch.

"Class consciousness rears its ugly head," he said as he extracted a pair of latex gloves from his pocket. "I'm going to take a closer look at the woman."

"Good idea," Munch said. Unlike his fellow detectives, he had brought an umbrella with him and was standing underneath it looking irritatingly dry. "She has nice pins, or have you already checked them out?"

Pembleton didn't bother answering. He moved around the victim, crouching a little, Bayliss at his side. Both men were very cautious about where they stepped, avoiding the wide puddles of mingled blood and rain on the sidewalk around her body.

The first thing that struck Pembleton as he studied her face, or what was left of it, was her expression. The gaping mouth with its peeled-back lips, the flared nostrils, the right eye opened wide to the stormy darkness. An expression of fear and shock. Naturally. She had not gone out walking her dog expecting a gunman to steal her life.

" 'The sword without, and the terror within,' " he said in a barely audible voice.

A passage from the Old Testament . . . the book was Deuteronomy, he remembered. . . . Deuteronomy 32, in which God takes insult at man's works and warns of his inescapable wrath.

" 'I will hide my face from them, I will see what their end shall be,' " he said, a bitter edge in his voice.

Bayliss regarded him for a long moment. Frank Pembleton—*Francis Xavier* Pembleton, as he had been christened by the Jesuit brothers who raised him from infancy with military drill and discipline— considered himself a fallen Catholic. Not *lapsed* but fallen. The difference, he had once explained, was that the former status resulted from neglect and laziness, whereas the latter arose from his belief that God had turned away from His flock, given up on them, left them foundering in the darkness without guidance or answers. That He no longer listened to their prayers, or cared about the terrible pain they inflicted on each other.

It had gotten so Pembleton claimed to feel that

nothing would ever change for the better, that the violence and suffering would go on and on regardless of how many murderers he brought down. . . .

But I have to keep trying, he had told Bayliss. For his wife, Mary, for his daughter, Olivia. Because if God had abandoned them . . .

Bayliss could recall his exact words . . .

If God has abandoned them to a world where crime goes unpunished, where there's no protection for the innocent, then damn God, damn Him to hell, I won't.

His exact words, and Bayliss thought he understood exactly what he had meant. They had worked together a lot of years now, these two men, and after all the cases they had investigated, hundreds and hundreds of cases, the messy wreckage of what had once been a human being rarely disturbed them anymore. A slug hit somebody in the face at 700 m.p.h., nobody expected the result to be pretty.

It was what *couldn't* be seen, the life that had departed the torn and bloodied remains, that never stopped crying out to them.

They stood beside each other, Pembleton a thinnish black man of thirty-five in a dripping-wet trenchcoat and grey fedora, Bayliss a white man of approximately the same age who appeared ten years younger until you looked into his haunted, careworn eyes, both of them staring down at the body of a dead woman in the steady rain.

"Has *anybody* seen the M.E.?" Pembleton was shouting to whoever happened to be within earshot.

"Cool it, Detective, I'm right here."

He looked over his shoulder to where Julianna Cox, who was not merely the medical examiner, but the *chief* medical examiner, was pushing her way toward him through the mass of police personnel. Dark-haired, pretty, with intense, deep-set brown eyes, she stood as tall as he did in the low-heeled boots she usually wore on the job, making her something like five-nine or five-ten, a striking height for a woman whose forceful personality alone was enough to command the attention of the men she worked with.

"I've been waiting—"

"And I've been busy bagging and tagging," she interrupted.

Pembleton frowned. Who would have ever guessed he'd find himself yearning for the days when Harry Scheiner had been dispatched to nine out of ten crime scenes? Once upon a time an assistant medical examiner like Scheiner would handle all except the high-profile cases from start to finish, but after the allegations of slipshod evidence collection those West Coast shysters had made—and in some humiliating instances successfully demonstrated—during the trial of their wealthy, murdering client, every big city police department from New York to La-la Land was playing it safe by sending out their top guns whenever possible.

"Okay, let's start over," Pembleton said. "I can see the cause of death was multiple gunshot wounds. I'm assuming the manner was homicide. What else do you have?"

"The victim was shot at point-blank range . . .

22

whoever killed her literally got right in her face," Cox said. She gestured toward a pair of techs squatting by a shop window some thirty or forty yards down the block. "They found a slug embedded in the brick facing of that storefront just millimeters above street level. I'm not a ballistics expert, but I do know that a bullet hitting a flat, hard surface will travel right along it rather than ricochet up."

"Meaning the gun was aimed straight down at the sidewalk when that shot was fired."

She nodded.

"Also meaning the woman was on the ground at that point, in which case the shooter must have intended to finish her off."

"I'm sticking to the basic science," Cox said, shrugging. "The rest is your job."

Pembleton grunted.

"Another thing," Cox said. "The murder weapon was a .22 LR automatic."

Pembleton furrowed his brow.

"Uncommon," he said.

"Very," she said.

He grunted again. "That all there is?"

"So far, yes," she said. "We'll keep looking for trace evidence on the victim, but I doubt there was any transference of hair or fiber. As far as I know the killer didn't actually make physical contact."

"Okay, thanks," Pembleton said. "Any objection to my examining the body now?"

"Be my guest," she said. "Just holler for me when you're finished."

Pembleton moved back toward the dead woman again. He found Bayliss squatting over her on the balls of his feet, his elbows on his knees, his hands linked under his chin.

"She's still holding her groceries," Bayliss said to him, indicating the plastic bags in her lifeless fingers. "They've got the name of the gourmet shop down the block printed on them." He shook his head. "One minute she's planning her dinner, the next—*pow*—good-bye."

Pembleton said nothing. He let his eyes make a slow pass over the body, wanting to observe what he could. He had noticed the groceries in her left hand as well as the leather handbag strapped over her right shoulder, and was thinking it very much resembled one that Mary had gotten herself a while back. She'd had a half-guilty look on her face for hours after she brought it home from the store, and though Pembleton hadn't really cared how much she'd spent on it, he'd supposed it must have cost quite a bit. The dead woman's too, judging by its appearance. Which led him to wonder if robbery might be eliminated as the motive here. A woman carrying an expensive-looking handbag, it made sense to assume she would have some money in it. Credit cards, maybe. Yet her assailant, who'd paused long enough to deliver the *coup de grace,* had apparently made no attempt to snatch it away from her.

Why had she been killed, then?

He carefully moved closer to the dead woman, reached for the handbag, and slid it down off her shoulder. It was styled something like a briefcase and had a clasp on the top flap. Balancing it on his knees, he opened the flap, dipped his gloved hand into the bag, and pored through its contents for something that might provide him with identification. After a few moments he took out a small leather cardholder and passed it over to Bayliss.

"Do us the honors," he said.

Bayliss opened the case, and almost immediately found a driver's license behind its clear plastic window.

"The victim's name is Donna Anne MacIntyre," he said, displaying the license in the pale-blue throw of a street lamp. "Date of birth, May 23, 1969. Address, 25 Hester Street."

"That's Scottish," Munch said from behind them.

"Huh?"

"The name. MacIntyre. Derived from the Gaelic *Mac-an-t-saoir,* meaning 'son of the carpenter.'"

Bayliss looked at him.

"Clan tartan's a blue and green plaid, with some red and white cross-stitching," Munch said.

"Jesus, how do you *know* all this stuff?"

"My intellect romps freely through the vast realms of human knowledge, plucking up facts like luscious grapes off the vine."

"*Useless* facts."

"You never can tell, Timmy."

Bayliss sighed and turned his eyes back to the photo on the license, comparing it to the gruesomely shattered face of the dead woman lying in front of him.

She had been very pretty. Beautiful, even. He wondered if the man to blame for murdering her had wanted to make certain that beauty was destroyed.

He put the driver's license back where he'd found it, pulled several credit cards from the slots inside the case, and looked them over.

Among them was a corporate security ID, the sort of swipe card used in many office buildings.

"Seems Donna worked for an outfit called Durham, Jellersen & Fisk," he said. He rubbed his chin. "That rings a bell."

"Sounds like a law firm," Pembleton said.

"Close, but no Macanudo," Munch said. "It's an upstart brokerage house based in New York. Made headlines this year for outperforming some of the old guard heavyweights on Wall Street."

Pembleton and Bayliss both looked at him.

"I read the financial rags," he said. "Like I said, you never can tell."

"The address on her license is only a couple of blocks away," Pembleton said. "One of us ought to head over there and see if anybody has to be notified."

"I'll do it," Munch said. "My glasses are starting to fog out here anyway."

Pembleton rose from his crouch.

"Okay," he said with a small nod of appreciation that caught Munch by surprise. "Bayliss and I are going to stick around and take statements."

"Meet you at the station," Munch said. "Save me some coffee if you get back before I do."

Pembleton nodded again.

Munch closed his umbrella long enough to slip under the crime scene tape, popped it open again on the other side, and walked off into the pouring rain.

Pembleton watched him go, and after a moment or two turned to Bayliss.

"We'd better talk to those witnesses before they get washed away," he said, brushing water off his sleeve.

The first person Pembleton interviewed was Betty Li Joong, a short, skinny, gray-haired woman whose family owned and operated the Korean grocery about halfway down the block from where the shooting had occurred.

"She walk by with dog," Mrs. Joong told him in badly broken English. "I inside store, see her through window."

They stood between the fruit and vegetable stands flanking the grocery's entrance, sheltered from the rain by a makeshift awning Mrs. Joong's son had fashioned by throwing a tarp over a wooden frame on the sidewalk. The big green sheet of plastic was keeping them more or less dry, the only problem being that its overhanging edges kept flapping in the gusty wind, flinging cold splashes of rainwater down the back of Pembleton's neck.

"Was she alone?"

"Except for little dog," she said. "Steady customer, come in twice week, maybe more. She stop in front of store, I think maybe going to buy something."

"Did she?"

Mrs. Joong looked at him blankly.

"Did she *buy* anything from you?" Pembleton clarified.

"Ah, no," she said. "When dog start to bark, she keep walking."

"Did she seem nervous in any way? Frightened?"

She shook her head.

"Do you remember if she was walking fast or slow?"

"Just *walking,*" she said, and shrugged.

"Not in any kind of hurry, then."

"No."

"As far as you could tell, was there anything *at all* unusual about the way she was acting?"

She thought a moment, then shook her head again.

"Mrs. Joong, do you recall ever seeing the woman come in with anyone else, a boyfriend maybe. . . ?"

She shrugged and spread her hands in front of her.

"Does that mean you might have?"

"I very busy," she said. "Too busy to watch customers all the time."

Pembleton didn't press. She was still shaken from what had happened, and he figured her recollection might improve after she'd had a chance to calm down.

"Okay," he said. "You mentioned that her dog was barking . . . do you have any idea why?"

"Always when she go into stores on block, she tie dog to parking meter. Come back out, dog happy."

"So what you heard was a *happy* bark?" Pembleton said, feeling kind of foolish as the question left his mouth.

Mrs. Joong nodded.

"And does that mean you saw nothing out of the ordinary about the *dog's* behavior, either?" he asked. In for an inch, in for a yard.

She hesitated a moment.

"Ma'am?"

"Not *see,*" she said finally, and touched a finger to her ear. "Maybe I *hear* something."

He looked at her. "What do you mean?"

"When woman in front of store, I taking care of customer at register," she said. "After she walk to corner, I hear dog make noise like it mad, want to bite somebody . . . how you say. . . ?"

She paused, groping for the correct word.

"Growling?" he asked. "Is that what it was doing?"

"Yes, yes."

"Let me make sure I understand you, Mrs. Joong," Pembleton said. "When you heard her dog make this growling sound, she'd already passed your store window, which means you didn't actually have a view of her anymore."

"Yes."

"But you knew it was *her* dog carrying on, and not somebody else's."

"Not know right away. Then somebody shoot gun. Five, six times. At first think kids playing with firecrackers, maybe break bottles. It very loud." She pressed her hand against her cheek as she spoke, clearly upset by the recollection. "When I hear gun, I go to door and look outside. Customer too. We see woman on sidewalk, dog next to her. "

"Still growling?"

"Yes."

"And the man who shot her?"

"Running away. Go to end of block, then turn around corner."

"So you never actually saw him fire the gun?"

"He running away," she repeated, shaking her head.

"Was there a weapon in his hand?"

"*Pistol,*" she said. "Hold it like so."

She shaped a gun with her right thumb and pointer finger and held it straight down against her thigh. Which, Pembleton thought worth noting, was how people with firearms training were taught to hold their guns when moving from an engagement . . . not that this would be a secret from anybody who'd ever watched a cop show on television.

"Mrs. Joong, can you describe the man with the gun for me?"

"Yes, I see him on street every day. A *bum.* He—"

"Wait a second," Pembleton interrupted. "Are you saying you think he's a homeless man?"

She nodded. "Sometimes he come in store, want me to give him food for nothing. Talk to himself like drunk or crazy."

"Is he white or black?"

"White."

"Tall, short?"

"Like you. Maybe little shorter."

"What else can you tell me about the way he looks?"

"Have long beard. Long hair, too."

"Is his hair straight or curly?"

30

She wobbled her hand.

"Wavy?"

"Yes, that right."

"What color is it? Brown, black, blond . . . ?"

"Brown, I think."

"You *think* or you're certain?"

"Brown, yes," she said, closing her eyes as if to picture him.

"How about his clothes? Can you describe what he was wearing tonight?"

"Always have on same thing. Green coat like soldier. Look old, many holes in it—"

"An *army* coat?"

"Yes. Army coat. And kind of hat that pull down over head."

"A knit cap."

"Yes. Dark color. Very dirty."

"How about the rest of his clothes?"

She shook her head to indicate she didn't recall.

"Did you notice whether he had any scars or other marks that could help to identify him?"

She shook her head.

"Okay, thank you very much." Pembleton switched off his tape recorder and returned it to his coat pocket. "I'll leave you my card so you can phone me if you remember anything else."

He handed it to her, and was starting toward the next witness, when she reached out from behind him and touched his arm.

"You going to find this man, officer?" she said, her eyes squarely meeting his own.

He stood there and looked back at her.

"I'm going to try," he said.

Robert Kessler was the customer who had been having his purchase rung up in the Korean grocery at the time of the shooting. A balding, somewhat overweight man of about forty in a Burberry trench coat and galoshes, he had stopped to pick up a few cans of baby formula on his way home from work, and was anxious to be on his way before his wife got the National Guard out looking for him.

As a matter of routine, Bayliss questioned him separately from Mrs. Joong. Every experienced cop knew that discrepancies were normal in statements taken at a crime scene, and that the best way to get at the truth of the occurrence in question was to compare the different versions and see where their particulars matched. When you kept witnesses in each other's presence, they tended, consciously or unconsciously, to alter their stories to make them agree, often blurring important details.

In the case of these two witnesses the accounts were quite close—a fact that would be a strong indication of their reliability when the detectives compared notes afterward.

Both Joong and Kessler had noticed the victim's dog barking playfully as she'd untied it from the meter, and then had suddenly heard the bark turn into an agitated growl after she started walking toward the corner. Moments later, both were startled by a series of popping sounds without first recognizing them as gunshots. Both told of hurrying outside to see what had made the noise, and of seeing Donna Anne MacIntyre sprawled in a pool of her own blood scarcely thirty feet from where they stood. Both saw a man fleeing from the body—and, most importantly, both described him as a homeless individual who had become something of a neighborhood fixture in recent months.

"He's been hanging around this block since the summer," Kessler said. "Maybe longer."

"You positive of that, huh?" Bayliss said.

"Of course." Kessler pouched his lip. "Why wouldn't I be?"

"I only ask because there are a lot of homeless in this city, and people very often don't notice them unless—"

"Unless they get right in your face," Kessler said. "Is that what you were about to say?"

Bayliss just shrugged.

"This guy's a real public nuisance," Kessler said. "Soldier of the Street."

"Excuse me?"

"That's what I call him, anyway."

"Because he wears an army jacket?"

"*And* carries a cardboard sign saying he's a Vietnam veteran who lost a kidney in the Tet Offensive, and needs carfare back to Minneapolis because his house burned down and a stray dog with hepatitis ate his wallet. You know, the typical hard luck story."

"I suppose," Bayliss said, jotting something into his

notebook. "Mr. Kessler, do you have any idea what this man's name might be?"

"It's not like he ever introduced himself to me."

"But maybe he gave his name to another person on the street, for instance. Or a storekeeper. What I'm asking is whether you might in passing have heard anybody else use it. . . ."

"No, never," Kessler said. "And even if I had, it'd probably be phony, wouldn't it?"

Bayliss shrugged noncommittally again.

"Well, I never said anything to him, or paid attention to anything he said to me, or listened to anything that might've been said between him and anybody else," Kessler said. "I try to mind my own business."

"What about the sign?"

"Huh?"

"The cardboard sign you mentioned," Bayliss said. "Is it possible he'd written his name on that?"

Kessler looked at him. "How should I know?"

"You just told me you'd read it. . . ."

"I was generalizing about what these *kinds* of signs say, not suggesting that I actually stop to read each and every one of them," Kessler said. "Please, Detective, I have a wife and hungry infant waiting at home, and I'd really like to get out of this deluge."

"I understand, we'll be through in a minute," Bayliss said. As if he actually *liked* standing out here in the rain. "Mr. Kessler, have you ever seen the man in the army coat get violent with anyone?"

"Well, I'd certainly consider shooting a person to death an act of violence—"

"Before tonight, that is," Bayliss said, wondering why people always acted as if they were obliged to be sarcastic with the police nowadays.

"No," Kessler said. "I mean, there were times when he'd be ranting and raving the way some of these guys do, but I couldn't tell you about what."

"No idea?"

"As I've already told you, I didn't pay attention."

Bayliss considered having Kessler go over his description of the shooter again, but decided that could wait for a follow-up interview . . . one that might best be conducted in a nice dry room at headquarters, and with a sketch artist present.

"Okay, that's all for now," he said. "I'll need a number where I can reach you in case there are any more questions."

"Sure," Kessler said, and gave it to him. "That's only if you need me, right?"

"Right."

"No offense, but I hope you don't," Kessler said.

Bayliss looked at him.

"I'll bet," he said.

A slender black man with a rainbow-striped fade, wearing a Speedo running suit and sneakers, Desmond Coates managed a beauty salon next door to the Korean grocer. He had also been drawn out into the street by the sound of gunshots only to see the assailant fleeing into the night.

". . . believe me, the guy's *psycho*," he was saying.

"How so?"

"Well, he's always talking to himself. . . . "

Pembleton heard a click from his tape recorder as it reached the end of a thirty-minute cassette, gestured for Coates to wait a moment, and flipped the tape over to its empty side.

"Okay, sorry for the interruption," he said, turning the machine back on. "About the man with the gun . . . can you tell me the sort of things he'd say when he talked to himself?"

"Tonight, you mean? Because I didn't even know he was hanging around the block tonight. Not until after I heard the shots."

"At *any* time, then."

"Oh, sure. He gets very loud, you know, and can come right up and shout in your face."

"And the things he says? . . ." Pembleton prompted, taking a third stab at what seemed to him like a very uncomplicated question.

"Mostly he carries on about the Vietnam war," Coates said. "How he was a special op, and used to go out with assassination squads in Cambodia and Laos—"

"Assassination squads?" Pembleton said. "Is that his term or yours?"

"Honey, I can't even tell you what it *means,*" Coates said. "He'd also say that he was going back to rescue the MIAs, and knew exactly where they were imprisoned, and would get even with the people in the government responsible for leaving them behind." He shrugged. "You've probably heard *that* part from a zillion other Rambos on the street."

Pembleton was thinking he had . . . but nine times out of ten these Rambos, as Coates called them, were as harmless as they were obnoxious.

"Sir, did this man ever seem dangerous to you?" he asked.

"You mean, other than screaming his head off and making my customers nervous?"

"I mean, were there occasions when he was *physically* threatening or aggressive?"

"Well, I'll tell you, I can live without the kind of free entertainment he provides," Coates said.

"Mr. Coates, specifically, have you ever seen him display a weapon of any type?"

"No," he said.

"Or damage any property?"

"No."

"Or actually attack someone before?"

Coates silently glanced up the block to where a couple of men in white were pushing the body of Donna Anne MacIntyre toward the morgue wagon atop a wheeled stretcher.

"No," he said. "But I guess there's a first time for everything."

"What I hear is *bang, bang, bang,*" Karim Hayes was telling Bayliss. A tall black kid of maybe seventeen wearing jeans and a hooded sweatshirt, he worked as a delivery boy for a take-out chicken shack around the corner, and had been riding past the scene on his bicycle when the shooting started. "Then she fall down on the sidewalk, an' Jake be standin' right over her—"

"Wait a second," Bayliss said. "You know the guy's *name?*"

"Name he go by on the street, anyway."

"You want to tell me *how* you know it?"

"Say it right on the sign he carry."

"The one about him being a homeless vet?"

"He always goin' on about the war," Hayes said, nodding.

"And the name, you're positive it's Jake?"

Hayes clucked his tongue in disgust. "I'm droppin' science here, man. You don't wanna believe me, that be your business."

"I'm just trying to get this right," Bayliss said. "So it's J-A-K-E?"

"You win the spellin' bee," Hayes said.

Bayliss wrote the information in his notebook, thinking Hayes riding by at the time of the killing might prove to be a tremendous stroke of luck, his attitude notwithstanding.

"Did you actually see him walk up to the woman and fire the gun?" he asked.

"Say I *hear* him first, you goan lissen or not?" Hayes said. "After she drop, that when I see Jake put the chrome right up to her face."

"And then?"

"Bang, bang, bang, bang, bang!"

"That's exactly five shots."

"Uh-huh."

"To her face."

"Got a feelin' you know *that* fo' you'self," Hayes said, and cocked his head toward the morgue wagon pulling away from the curb. "Them bullets do somethin' hideous to her."

Bayliss didn't comment. "Did you hear either of them say anything?"

"Think she be screamin', ain't sure what."

"You have any idea at all?"

"Sound like 'No, no, please,'" Hayes said. "Somethin' like that."

"Was this before or after you heard those first few gunshots?"

"Befo'," Hayes said.

"You sure?"

"Think I can't tell the difference?"

"Look, how about you take it easy. . . ."

Hayes pointed to his bike. "Don' know why I should, 'less you goan explain that basket fulla cold, wet chicken to my boss—"

"Okay, okay, I'll only keep you here another minute," Bayliss said, thinking. "This guy Jake . . . you never heard him ask the woman for money? Or anything else?"

"Nope."

"Did you *see* him try to take anything from her before he ran?"

"Like what?"

"I don't know," Bayliss said. "You're the witness."

"Yo, man, I'm tellin' you this wasn't nothin' like a rip-off. Jake do her stone-cold. Have his finger onna trigger alla way. "

Bayliss sighed.

"Okay, we're through for now," he said. "Thanks a lot."

Hayes stood watching him a moment. Then he clucked his tongue again and suddenly thrust out his hand. "You wanna lay a five on me, make up fo' the tips I lost?"

"Fat chance," Bayliss said, shutting his notebook.

Quickstepping through the rain, Munch found a match for the address on Donna Anne MacIntyre's driver's license on the awning of a new luxury apartment building near the waterfront. There was a lot of shiny brass around the glass entrance doors and a doorman stood in the carpeted vestibule. Munch flashed his shield as he was admitted, established that this was indeed Ms. MacIntyre's current residence, asked the doorman whether she lived alone or with a companion, and was told she was the only permanent occupant of her apartment, although her sister from out of town had been staying with her for about a month.

"You mind checking if anybody's home?" Munch asked.

"I can tell you right now—"

"Let me guess," Munch said. "Donna left here with her dog maybe an hour, an hour and a half ago."

The doorman eyed him curiously. "Walks her pooch the same time every night. . . . Ain't seen her come back yet, which is kind of odd."

"You'd better call upstairs," Munch said. He removed his eyeglasses, wiped splatters of rain off the

40

lenses with the arm of his coat, and slipped them back over his hawkish nose. "I need to talk to her sister."

"Sure, just a minute," the doorman said, and reached for his phone.

Munch waited, staring outside, watching the heavy rain smear the lights of passing cars over the big glass doors. He heard the doorman announce him, waited some more, and then was told he could go right upstairs, the apartment was 5F, just to the left of the elevators.

Donna's sister was a woman in her late twenties, Munch guessed, wearing a sleeveless wine-colored tee shirt, a short denim skirt over black exercise tights, and black mules. She was slim and tall, about five feet seven or eight, with a narrow, pretty face, light brown hair, and blue eyes that were open very wide, betraying her nervousness.

Munch identified himself from out in the corridor. "I'm sorry to disturb you," he said, "but are you—?"

"My name's Jessica. Jessica Andrews." She was examining his badge, reading the words engraved on the badge. "I don't understand. You—you're a *homicide* detective?"

He nodded. "If you don't mind, I need to talk to you."

"Certainly," she said, unlatching the door chain, letting him into the apartment.

He followed her into a living room filled with antique wooden furniture, glazed, fragile-looking Chinese vases, and several chairs and a sofa upholstered with a light floral fabric. On the wall opposite the sofa was a large abstract art print, luminous blossoms of white, orange, and red exploding in deep blue space.

Jessica noticed him studying the picture and said, "That's a Max Ernst. Well, a *reproduction* of one of his paintings. He was a Swedish artist, I think."

"German," Munch said. "And one of the first whose work was outlawed by the Nazis during World War Two."

She looked at him steadily. Anxiously.

"I'm surprised you've heard of him. . . . It isn't like he's a household name," she said and paused, her eyes asking the question she could not yet bring herself to voice. "Donna's a fanatic about his work. This one's called *Little Girls Set Out to Hunt the White Butterflies.*"

He nodded.

"It's always been her favorite," she said.

Watching him closely, still avoiding the unavoidable.

He nodded again, meeting her worried eyes with his own, both of them standing silently in front of the print.

"My sister," she said at last. Watching him, watching him. "Is something wrong?"

Munch inhaled. No matter how many times you did it, it was always hard. "I think you ought to sit down. . . ."

She moved toward a chair but just stood there beside it.

"Tell me," she said.

"Ma'am, a woman was shot to death a few blocks

away from here," he said. "She was walking a small brown dog—"

"Oh my God—"

"We believe her to be your sister Donna," he continued, getting it all said.

"My God," she repeated, her face going white, her lips trembling. She swayed a little and placed a hand on the armrest of the chair, steadying herself.

Munch started toward her. "You okay?"

She nodded and waved him away, finally sinking into the chair.

"Are—are you absolutely sure it's Donna?" she asked, shuddering. "I mean, she just went out to do some shopping. . . ."

"We're still not certain about the details, but it appears someone, a man with a gun, approached her on the street. . . ." He took another deep breath. "So far, it doesn't seem as if anything was stolen."

She looked up at him, the tears coming now, spilling down her cheeks.

"I don't understand," she said. "You mean *it wasn't a robbery?*"

Munch looked at her. They always wanted to know why their loved one was gone, wanted there to be a reason.

"We can't be sure," he said. "The person that did this ran off, and we haven't found him yet. Witnesses have told us he's a homeless man who's been seen around the neighborhood. It could be that he intended to grab her wallet and panicked before he got a chance.

43

As I said, it appears that the money and credit cards she was carrying were left behind."

She began to cry more heavily, sobbing, shaking her head. Munch reached into his coat pocket for a tissue, stepped forward to hand it to her, and then turned away as she nodded her thanks, giving her some room.

His eyes wandered to the print on the wall, the vivid splashes of brightness coalescing out of the dark. Looking at it made him feel sad, although he doubted that had been the artist's intent.

He turned back to Jessica.

"Ms. Andrews, I have to ask: have you noticed any suspicious people loitering outside this building lately?"

"No," she said in a choked voice.

"Anybody on the street or in the hallways . . . ?"

"No."

"Is there anyone at all you can think of who might've wanted to harm your sister?"

"You just said it was a vagrant—"

"According to several bystanders who saw the shooting, yes," he said. "But nothing's been confirmed at this point, and we don't want to ignore any possibilities."

She was looking up at him, the tissue bunched in her hand, smears of mascara around her eyes. Until now, he hadn't realized she was wearing makeup.

"I can't think of anyone," she said.

"Nobody with whom she'd had personal problems?"

"I'm not sure I understand what you mean," she said.

He took in a deep breath. "Maybe this isn't the best time—"

"No, please," she said. "Go ahead."

"Well, frankly, I'm thinking about romantic involvements."

"Donna hasn't dated anyone since I came to stay with her, and that was back at the end of September."

"And before that?"

"I don't know," she said. "I . . . I'd been living in New York—that's where we're from originally—and was going through a rough divorce. The last few months before I came down here, when we talked on the phone it was mostly about that. What was happening in my life, I mean. I was really at loose ends, and we both kind of decided it'd be a good idea if I gave Baltimore a try. . . ." She shook her head. "I knew Donna went out with people, but she hasn't had a serious relationship for years. She's—she was very engaged in her career."

Munch considered a moment. "Your sister worked at Durham, didn't she?"

She looked surprised.

"There was a corporate ID card among the things in her wallet," he explained.

"Oh," she said. "Of course. . . ."

"To your knowledge, had Donna been having any difficulties at work?"

She shook her head, wiping tears off her face. "Just the opposite. There was an article about her in *Trend-setter* a couple of months ago. Her picture was on the cover of the magazine."

"Would I be able to see a copy?"

She nodded. "There's one in Donna's bedroom. I'll try to find it for you."

"I appreciate it."

"But why . . . ?"

"I'm just trying to be thorough," he said, supposing it was possible some nutjob could have recognized her face from the cover of the magazine and acted out a violent fantasy by killing her. Could have even been stalking her and waiting for the right opportunity to strike.

He filed that thought away for the moment and picked up on another one that had occurred to him. "Ma'am, you mentioned your divorce. . . ."

"My ex-husband's very happy in Santa Fe with his brand new wife and baby," she said, and was suddenly crying hard again. "Greg had no grudge against Donna—he doesn't even know I moved here. The alimony checks go to a post office box in New York."

Munch dropped the matter. The bitter emotion in her voice had made him feel awkward and intrusive. But there was something else he had to ask of her.

He sighed. No sense putting it off.

"I know this won't be easy, Ms. Andrews . . . but we need to have a family member identify your sister's body."

She looked at him, looking pulverized, her eyes red and puffy.

"She was brought to the coroner's laboratory pending an autopsy, and it would be best if this were taken care of as soon as possible," he said.

Silence. And more silence. He did nothing to rush her.

"I'll find that magazine for you and then get my coat," she said finally, rising from her chair. "It won't take long."

"Thank you," Munch said, and a moment later was left alone in the room.

Waiting, he absently glanced around at the arrangement of delicately painted Chinese vases, the elegant wooden furniture, but stopped his eyes from returning to the print on the wall.

Somehow, it depressed him too much to look at it.

THREE

GENERALLY WHEN THE heater worked, the power windows stuck. Or if *they* worked, the windshield wipers didn't—and here Pembleton felt it was important to note that he was not only driving in the rain without *working* wipers, but without any wipers at all, as if they'd been cannibalized for installation on another vehicle.

"Why do that?" he thought aloud. "How does someone decide what parts to remove, and which cars to put them in?"

Beside him in the passenger seat, Bayliss said nothing.

"It might be understandable if each car were permanently assigned to an individual detective," Pembleton went on. "A creature of low cunning like Gaffney, for example, could have a mechanic in his pocket. But nobody can possibly know in advance which car they're going to get . . . or can they?"

Silence from Bayliss.

Pembleton glanced over at him and frowned. He had brought his playing cards out of his pocket and was intently manipulating them with one hand.

"Nice that you're listening to me," Pembleton said.

"Huh?"

"Never mind." Pembleton steered the car.

"I was practicing my manual artifice, Frank," Bayliss said.

"What?"

"Sleight of hand," Bayliss said. "It's the purest form of magic."

"That so?"

"Sure. And the most introverted. No assistants, no props to lug around. Somebody asks to see a trick, you reach for your deck and do it."

"Oh."

"It's kind of like being a stand-up comedian. The best ones don't need dummies or suitcases full of goofy rubber fish. They rely on their natural wit."

"Oh."

"Incidentally, the sleight I'm doing now is called a 'little-finger break,'" he said. "Though the thumb's involved, too."

Pembleton drove. The road seemed to have smudged across the rain-coated windshield. He squinted into the flowing night and wondered what the hell had gotten into Bayliss lately.

"What the hell's gotten into you lately?" he said.

Bayliss held the pack out as if a spectator—an invisible leprechaun, maybe—was sitting atop the dash, and then began moving the cards about with his fingertips.

"Don't you like to be fooled?" he said.

Pembleton looked blank. He hated it when people responded to one question with another.

"No," he said flatly. "I do not."

Bayliss produced a disbelieving laugh.

"Oh come on, Frank," he said. "Everybody does."

"I just told you, I don't."

"How about surprise parties?" Bayliss said. "Didn't anybody ever throw you one?"

"No," Pembleton said. "And if someone did, I'd probably never speak to him again."

Bayliss sighed. "You get a kick out of big-budget special-effects movies?"

"Not particularly."

"Amusement parks? Disneyland?"

"No," Pembleton said.

"Okay, I quit," Bayliss said, frustrated. "If you aren't going to admit—"

"I don't enjoy being fooled, deceived, misled, or in any way duped," Pembleton said. "Which, come to think of it, might be among the reasons I became a detective."

"You're confusing two different issues," Bayliss said. "I'm not talking about getting fooled when it comes to *serious* things. This is about entertainment. Even novelists try to fool their readers."

"How's that?"

"I dunno, exactly, but some famous mystery writer

said it on a talk show I was watching the other day," Bayliss said.

A traffic light shifted from green to yellow to red ahead of them. Pembleton slowed to a halt, the car's tires shedding water on the blacktop.

"Look, Frank, we've been partners for five years now," Bayliss said. "In that time how many murders have we worked? Two hundred? Three hundred?"

"Something like that," Pembleton said.

"And out of those cases, how many were multiples?"

Pembleton shrugged. "I'd guess maybe a third of them."

"So that's, what, a minimum of four hundred dead bodies, and probably closer to a thousand. Men, women, little *kids,*" Bayliss said, shaking his head. "We've seen them sliced, diced, and ventilated with bullet holes—and that's before we watch them get cut up on the coroner's slab like Christmas hams."

Pembleton didn't see how that had anything to do with what they were talking about.

"How's that have anything to do with what we're talking about?" he asked.

"Far as I'm concerned, it's got everything to do with it." Bayliss accidentally dropped a card to the floor of the car and bent to pick it up. "Still don't have this palming bit down," he muttered.

The light turned green. Pembleton tapped the gas pedal with his foot and the car swished forward through the rain.

"Think about the fresh one we were looking at ten minutes ago," Bayliss said. "Donna Anne MacIntyre.

Some guy goes and shoots the poor woman, turns her head to pulp, and Munch is standing there and giving us the historical origins of her name. And that's after he's already made comments about her legs." He paused. "Be totally honest with me, Frank. Did *you* notice her legs?"

Pembleton hesitated.

"Yes," he said, "I did."

"And so did I," Bayliss said. "But what's that say about us? The woman's *deceased*. You gotta wonder if we're normal."

"She had good legs," Pembleton said. "It was just an observation. We spend a lot of time looking at dead bodies, and the fact that we're used to it doesn't make us necrophiles."

"That's my point," Bayliss said. "You do police work, death goes with the terrain. It doesn't shock you anymore."

"So what you're getting at is that we need some kind of escape from reality," Pembleton said. "Which I assume you've found through doing card tricks."

Bayliss shook his head.

"You've got it backwards," he said.

"Backwards?"

"Right," Bayliss said. "The thing I like is figuring out the reality behind the deception and maybe having some control over it. For a change."

"I don't—"

A cat suddenly appeared in the middle of the street and Pembleton slammed the brake, almost running it over. He watched the startled animal dart between two parked cars and expelled a long breath. Probably he'd have seen it sooner if there had been goddamned wipers on the car.

Somebody honked his horn behind him and he drove on.

"Sorry," he said, noticing that Bayliss had spilled his cards all over his lap when he'd pulled the short stop.

"It's okay." Bayliss was busy reassembling the deck. "Things happen."

"You going to finish explaining about the connection between card tricks and what we do?"

"Maybe later," he said. They were less than a block from headquarters and he could see the building's large, fortresslike outline coming up on the left. "I'm kinda anxious to talk to Munch about what he found out."

Pembleton was thinking that he really didn't feel like waiting for the explanation.

"Sure, it can wait," he said.

And, mindful of the pouring rain and his lack of an umbrella, he began to search for a parking space near the station's front door.

"So," Giardello said, his voice booming vigorously, "can I assume you've brought in our perpetrator, along with the unimpeachable evidence that will assure the district attorney of a conviction?"

It was a little past nine o'clock at night and he was in his office with Pembleton, Bayliss, and Munch, the four men having assembled there for a meeting about the newly underway MacIntyre investigation. In the picture frames on the desk in front of him, right where he could see them, snapshots of his long-deceased wife and three grown daughters offered windows into sentiments that Giardello rarely exposed otherwise. In the glass case on the wall immediately behind him, dozens of neatly mounted BCPD patches conveyed his absolute devotion to the fraternity of police officers and his equally unfailing commitment to the job of protecting the innocent and apprehending the guilty within the margins of the law.

To regard it as symbolic that Lieutenant Al Giardello had made his place between these reminders of his family and emblems of the department would not have been terribly farfetched . . . not at all, in fact.

Family.

The department.

From where he sat, they were the things that truly mattered.

"Why the dead silence?" he asked, watching the faces of his detectives.

"Chief," Pembleton ventured tentatively, "it's only been two hours since we caught the squeal."

"Bah!" Giardello said, sounding like Leo G. Carroll portraying an evil mastermind. "That's two hours the killer's been at large somewhere." He tented his hands under his chin. "Tell me what leads you've got," he said.

And waited.

"Well, according to maybe five eyewitnesses the shooter's a homeless guy with head problems," Bayliss said, and filled him in about the so-called Soldier of the Streets. "You ask me, this one won't be too complicated."

"Was the gun recovered?"

"Well, no," Bayliss said. "But—"

"Was anything stolen?"

"Apparently not," Pembleton said. "Although—"

"So what's the theory of the crime?"

They looked at him.

"Do we *have* a theory?" he asked.

"It was a random attack by a crazy. Period," Pembleton said. He was standing to the left of the desk, hands in the pockets of his open trench coat. "These things happen."

Giardello grunted. "The witnesses to the shooting," he said. "Have you put them together with a sketch artist so we can work up a composite of the suspect?"

Pembleton and Bayliss exchanged glances.

"We thought we'd set up appointments with them tomorrow," Pembleton said. "Most of the people we talked to were on the way home from work or—"

"Balderdash!" Giardello said, sounding even more like a celluloid character from the thirties than before. Munch wondered if he'd recently gotten into watching black and white flicks on cable television. "You should have brought all of them here right away."

Pembleton didn't tell his boss he disagreed with that. In his experience, a bunch of soggy and tired witnesses would be far less cooperative than ones who'd had a good night's sleep, and since none of them were likely to disappear in this instance, why not give them a break?

"Okay," Giardello said, letting the matter go. "Have you located any members of the victim's family yet?"

Yes, they had, the detectives told him, with Munch explaining that he'd just sent Jessica Andrews home in a patrol car after she'd confirmed the body was indeed that of her sister Donna. He then quickly summarized what he'd learned while visiting the dead woman's apartment.

"Donna Anne MacIntyre had made a big splash in the market," he said, holding up the issue of *Trendsetters* with the feature article about her. "Her sister gave me this magazine before we left her place."

The other detectives studied it in silence. The cover presented Donna Anne standing beside a wall-sized financial chart in a smart business suit, her blond hair cut in a neat wedge, looking pretty, intelligent, and capable.

"I'm afraid that she's about to make another, even bigger splash," Giardello said. "The press is going to have a ball with this story. Sexy female executive slain in random attack. A life of promise cut short by a homeless man. It's the sort of thing news reporters love—and I'm talking nationwide."

"Maybe we can play the media attention to our advantage," Pembleton said. "Put our sketch of the suspect out on TV and the front pages. It's almost a sure bet somebody will recognize him on the sidewalk, a park bench, or whatever."

"Assuming the sketch ever gets done," Giardello grumbled. He looked thoughtfully at Munch. "You say

Jessica Andrews told you her sister wasn't having personal problems?"

"None that she knew of, anyway," Munch said.

"Why waste time with that angle?" Pembleton said. "There are plenty of people who scoped the murderer as a neighborhood wacko. It's open and shut."

"Probably," Giardello said. "But nobody gets anywhere in this world without making somebody else angry or jealous. I still want one of you to go see the people she worked with. Let them tell you directly how everything was hunky-dory. Just to be thorough."

"I'll talk to them," Munch said. "Being that I'm the squad's resident financial expert."

"What about you two?" Giardello asked, his eyes alternating between Pembleton and Bayliss.

"Soon as the composite's ready tomorrow, we'll start our canvass, show the drawing around to people in the area," Pembleton said. "Including street people."

"We can hit food lines, public shelters, places like that," Bayliss added. "Like Frank said, somebody's bound to make him."

Giardello didn't answer right away.

"Okay," he said finally. "It seems to me that we know where we're going. But I want this case resolved fast. The longer it drags on, the brighter the spotlight will be. And I intensely dislike standing in it." He grunted again. "Anything else?"

"I could give you some free advice about managing your portfolio," Munch said.

Giardello pointed toward the door.

"Take *my* advice and get out of here," he said. "Right now."

FOUR

AT 1:00 P.M. ON Wednesday, the day after Donna Anne MacIntyre was killed, Bayliss found himself standing over a hillock of sodden, outspread sheets of newspaper and rain-soaked woolen blankets, trying to ascertain whether a human being was somewhere at the bottom of it, and, assuming someone actually *was* down there, to determine if that person was awake or merely feigning sleep so that he would quit trying to initiate contact and go away.

"I'm a detective with the police department—can you *hear* me?" he said in a loud voice, leaning over and cupping his hands around his mouth like a referee at a sporting event.

This was the third time he'd identified himself and then asked that question. Once more and he figured he'd have to start excavating the wet mound of old covers and yesterday's headlines layer by layer.

Fortunately, it shifted just enough to satisfy Bayliss he'd communicated with the Spirit of the Mountain.

"Come on," he said, and tentatively reached down to shake whoever was buried in that sopping, unpleasant heap. "I don't want to be out on the sidewalk all afternoon."

"You think I *do?*" a muffled female voice said from below. "It's been comin' down in buckets."

Bayliss didn't see how he could argue with that. Unless he chose to point out that, the depressing overcast aside, a lull in the storm system passing over the mid-Atlantic had allowed Baltimore and its surrounding counties to surface from underwater . . . if only temporarily, according to the forecasters.

"Look, I'm not trying to hassle anybody," he said after a moment. "All I want is to ask you a few questions."

A corner of the blanket flapped back to reveal a mat of dark hair, two rheumy red eyes, and a wrinkled face the color of mummy wrappings.

"You sayin' this ain't a roust?" she asked, her mouth still hidden under the blankets.

"No, no. Just take a look at this for me."

He reached into his coat pocket for his photocopy of the composite drawing that had been rendered of Jake, Soldier of the Street.

"This guy look familiar?" he asked, showing it to her.

She shrugged a little further out of her soiled cocoon of blankets and newspapers, raised herself on her elbows, and examined the drawing.

It had taken most of the morning to corral the witnesses to the MacIntyre shooting and put them together with a sketch artist at headquarters—in part because Mr. Kessler, who worked in the marketing department of a direct-sales cosmetics outfit, had been mulishly uncooperative when Bayliss phoned him at his office, making Bayliss swear up and down that the police would be through with him by eleven so that he could attend a noon luncheon with somebody from QVC, and then continuing to hedge despite the endless guarantees. He'd finally relented after Bayliss tossed him an extra bone, promising that a team of uniformed officers would pick him up, wait for him to finish giving his input to the sketch artist, and afterward drive him to the restaurant where he was having his business lunch. Kessler had seemed particularly attracted to the idea of the television guy seeing him arrive in a patrol car, which did not at all surprise Bayliss. He'd marked him from the beginning as the type that liked being made to feel important.

In sharp contrast, Betty Li Joong, Desmond Coates, and the handful of others who had seen the shooter were far less reluctant to help with the artist's workup, and even Karim Hayes, the fried chicken delivery boy, had offered nary a word of complaint when he was asked to come to the station, having had nothing else to do with himself anyway.

"Quit my job lass night," he'd explained. "Decided I was tired a' workin' outdoors."

By eleven o'clock, the sketch had been completed and Xeroxed in multiple, after which Bayliss and

Pembleton had decided to save time by splitting the legwork between them, with Pembleton visiting places that offered food, beds and medical treatment to the homeless, and Bayliss hitting the streets to see what he could turn up.

Now he waited some more as the woman studied the drawing in his hands, letting her get a good look at it. She was situated at the mouth of a narrow alley running alongside a trendy retro-clothing shop (the term *antique* clothing, which had replaced the term *recycled* clothing, which had replaced the term *used* clothing, now being nearly obsolete itself) about three blocks from where the slaying had taken place. Bayliss wondered if the dirty, ragged mackinaw she was wearing qualified as retro. He also wondered if the suspect's own mother would be able to recognize him from the nondescript features on the sketch. The nose and mouth were neither large nor small, the neck neither long nor short, the shoulders neither broad nor narrow. A full beard hid his cheeks and any identifying marks that might be on them. Besides the beard and his long hair, he had no outstanding features, at least in the artist's sketch Bayliss was carrying around with him. And what else could have been expected? The thing about the homeless was that they were largely invisible until they began acting in a conspicuous or aggressive manner. Which, when you thought about it, only gave people more reason to avoid looking at them.

A car swooped past the curb on the cobblestone

street behind Bayliss, splashing water from a backed-up sewer all over his coat.

He decided to nudge the woman along.

"So," he said, "you know this man?"

She responded with an indeterminate grunt.

"That mean you do or you don't?"

Her runny eyes studied him. "Could be a lotta guys," she said, none to his surprise. "How come you're lookin' for him?"

"A woman was shot in the neighborhood last night, and we think he can help us find out who did it," he said, figuring that was telling her enough. "Any particular reason you're interested?"

She shrugged. "I try'n be careful. Know who's trouble an' who ain't. Out here on the street, what you don't know can get you hurt."

Bayliss said nothing. He was thinking how he'd been able to feel winter in the air for the past few days, the rain, fog and clouds having stolen what little warmth was left to the season. He was also thinking that this woman was probably sixty, sixty-five years old. Right around his mother's age. The combination of these thoughts somehow embarrassed him. And left him feeling even gloomier than he'd already felt thanks to the dismal weather.

"You got anythin' else besides the picture?" she asked.

"What do you mean?"

"I mean like his name. Or if he got a funny way-a walkin'. Like that."

"He calls himself Jake," Bayliss said. "And he's a

disabled Vietnam vet. Or says he is, anyway. Been in this area more or less since the summer."

The expression that came over her face told Bayliss something had clicked.

"What is it?" he asked. "You're looking like maybe you remember the guy."

"Maybe I do," she said, and eyed him suspiciously. "What kinda trouble you say he's in?"

"I didn't," he said. "But it's very important that we talk to him. So certain things can be cleared up."

She grunted again. "Still ain't sure I oughtta tell you anything. Gotta protect ourselves out here. Nobody else gonna do it."

"Look, someone killed an innocent woman," Bayliss said, getting impatient. "That person's a threat to everybody around."

She stared at him.

"Well?" he said.

"I know him," she said finally, and sat up a little more. "Except he told me his name was Rich. We sorta stayed together for a few days back when it was hot out. Must've been around August."

"I'm not exactly sure I understand," he said. "When you say 'stayed together' . . . ?"

"It's like I told you, we got to take care-a each other out here. My leg gives me problems. Swells up somethin' awful, especially when the weather gets real hot or cold. One day Rich sees me, asks if maybe I need some help, and I tell him yeah."

"Had you known him before that time?"

"No, an' that didn't make any difference. My

goddamn leg was hurtin' so bad I could hardly walk across the street," she said. "Gave him money to buy us some food, an' something for his thirst."

"Booze, you mean?"

"That's right," she said. "He was a drinker."

"You ever notice him get violent with people, hear voices, anything odd like that?"

"Not so far as I can remember, but who knows?" she said. "He didn't stick around more'n a couple days."

"Any special reason?"

"My money ran out," she said with a small, drab smile. "Chicken one day, feathers the next."

He folded the composite back up and returned it to his pocket.

"You see Rich, or Jake, or whatever his name is, around lately?"

"Once in a while," she said. "Sometimes he goes to those free suppers at the St. Ignatius church. They have 'em every day. I mighta seen him there."

Bayliss nodded. He was pretty sure St. Ignatius was on Pembleton's list of outreach centers.

"That it?"

She appeared to be concentrating. "Seen him on the street with a guy named Ossie a few times. Couldn't tell you when."

"What's this Ossie look like?"

"He's a young black kid. Real skinny. Got this big mark on his cheek looks like an ink spot." She paused, added, "Think Ossie's into the crack."

"You have any idea where I can find him?"

"Somewhere between land, sea, and sky."

Bayliss looked at her.

"Think you can be more specific?"

"Try that new building over by the water on Grant Street," she said. "It's got one-a them indoor malls. Lotta guys hang around there."

Bayliss thanked her, started to turn away, hesitated.

"You going to be okay?" he asked.

"Sure," she said. "A hunnerd dollar bill'd make me even more okay, though."

He reached into his pocket for his wallet.

"You'll have to settle for a twenty," he said.

A gray stone church without elaborate woodwork or ornamentation, St. Ignatius had an air of honest strength that very much appealed to Pembleton, and he paused there on the way to the connected rectory, admiring it, climbing to the top of its wide front steps, standing in the entrance and looking past the vestibule to the dark, silent, silent pews, the long nave leading up to the crossing, and the Communion rail with the simple wood altar behind it. . . .

Standing there . . .

Standing in the entrance of the big, empty church with his solitary memories of the Jesuit mission where he'd been raised, attending morning service and vespers each weekday, giving confession on Saturday, and taking Communion on Sunday, his heart stirred by the sermon and Mass, his head upturned to receive the sacramental wafer, bread of angels, Body and Blood of Christ, o Lord, o blessed Lord, how safe he had felt back then, how young and secure in his faith . . .

and how terribly, immeasurably distant those feelings seemed to him now.

Pembleton smoothed his trench coat down along his arms and turned back toward the street. This would be his fourth stop that afternoon and he wasn't even halfway through his list of homeless centers.

Better not waste any more time.

He descended the stairs, went on to the modest structure where the priest resided, rang the doorbell, and waited. The man who answered was dark-haired and in his midforties, wearing gray flannel pants and a clerical collar under a white shirt and herringbone blazer. He looked at Pembleton's shield and identification with some perplexity, introduced himself as Father Joseph Donnelly, led him into a tidy, wood-paneled office, and nodded toward a chair.

"What can I do for you, Detective Pembleton?" he asked, sitting across the desk from him.

Pembleton got straight to it, telling the priest he was investigating a murder that was believed to have been committed by a homeless man, showing him the composite sketch of the suspect, and explaining that, as St. Ignatius was known to operate a soup kitchen and other assistance programs for the needy, it was hoped someone at the parish might recognize him from the drawing.

Donnelly's face was sober. He listened quietly while Pembleton spoke, then said, "We feed over a hundred and fifty men and women every night on average. I try to get to know as many of them as possible, but . . ."

He shrugged, letting the sentence hang.

"You're saying you don't recall seeing him here?" Pembleton said.

"I'm saying I can't be certain," he said, handing the sketch back to Pembleton.

Pembleton looked at him. "Am I picking up a touch of hostility, Father?"

Donnelly met his gaze and sighed.

"Hostility, no," he said. "Defensiveness, very possibly."

"You want to tell me why?"

Donnelly sighed again. "I heard about the murder on the radio this morning. It's the sort of tragedy that makes one feel helpless. Depressed. And, in my own case, worried."

Pembleton thought he understood.

"You're concerned about what public reaction could do to your program," he said.

Donnelly nodded.

"Its existence depends entirely upon donations of food, money, and clothing. If the community starts to think we're bringing dangerous maniacs to their streets, that's the end of their support. We'd be shut down in a matter of weeks."

"You really believe your backing's that fickle?"

"Frightened people can make hasty, unwise decisions."

"In which case you might want to consider how scared they'll get if there's another killing," Pembleton said.

Donnelly blanched. "I don't like what you're implying, Detective. Nothing could sadden me more than what happened to that poor woman. The day I become so cynical as to weigh the taking of a human life against some personal agenda, however passionate I may be about it, is the day I'll resign from the clergy."

"With all due respect, Father, it seems that's exactly what you're doing," Pembleton said. "You barely glanced at the drawing of the suspect. You've avoided the possibility that you even *might* be able to recognize him. And you've made it clear you don't want your church linked to the man who committed the murder last night." He looked sharply at Donnelly. "If that isn't saying the victim's of lesser value than the smooth operation of your program, I don't know what is."

Donnelly opened his mouth, closed it, cleared his throat.

"Detective Pembleton, the widespread perception is that most homeless people are dangerous lunatics, and that if they could only be hospitalized or jailed the problem of having them on our streets would be solved," he said. "It's a simplistic way of looking at a complex problem, and an excuse for ducking our moral responsibilities."

"All of which may be true," Pembleton said, "but—"

"Please let me finish," Donnelly interrupted, his voice tight. "Mental health facilities have obviously dumped millions of individuals into society without considering whether they would survive *or* present serious threats to others. But according to most studies the root causes of homelessness are economic. The lack of jobs and low-cost housing, urban redevelopment without regard for the people who are being displaced, the dismantling of the federal welfare system, all of it has a terrible impact on the poor and marginally poor." He paused. "Maybe we shouldn't be asking ourselves how many of the homeless are mentally ill, but how many of them go crazy from isolation and stress."

Pembleton waited until he was sure Donnelly was through talking, then slowly leaned forward.

"I'm here to track down a killer," he said, spacing his words. "Not discuss social problems."

Donnelly cleared his throat again. "If you saw what we do here on the front lines, maybe you'd understand. . . ."

"No," Pembleton said. "No, I wouldn't."

Donnelly straightened in his chair.

"Your suspect honestly doesn't look familiar to me," he said in a dismissive tone. "I wish I could be of more help."

Pembleton looked at him in silence for a moment, then stood up.

"Last I heard, Father, lying is still a venial sin," he said.

"And absolution a lasting hope for us all," Donnelly said.

The guy who'd climbed into the Dumpster outside the furniture store, name of Larry, had lived on the streets going on five years, a long time for sure. Although the guy who was waiting *next* to the Dumpster, his shopping cart full of plastic trash bags bulging with returnable cans and bottles—he went by the name of Jos—had been on the streets for over a decade. Or claimed he had, anyway.

Out here, you got used to hearing plenty of fiction.

"You find anything yet?" Jos asked, impatient. He wanted to get to the supermarket and trade in his returnables before the night manager came on shift at four. The night manager was a limpdick bastard. Let him get into one of his moods, and he'd give you some bullshit about the machine being out of change, show you the door before you could redeem a single fucking bottle.

"You wanna gimme a chance?" Larry said from inside the big commercial Dumpster. "I only been at it a couple minutes."

Jos sucked air into the space where his missing front teeth had been to signal his continued annoyance.

"Either you see a right-size box, or you don't," he said.

"See *lotsa* boxes that're the right size," Larry said. "Just no good ones."

"What's the difference?"

"You know the difference."

"You gonna start in about them Chinese boxes again?"

"Well, what can I say?"

"Jesus Christ."

"Gimme a Chinese box over an American box anytime," Larry said. "Ain't never seen a Chinese box fall apart inna rain."

"What about the one we was sleepin' in yesterday? Turned to fuckin' mush."

"I told you it wasn't Chinese."

"It said right on the flap that it was Chinese."

"I don't give a shit what it said; it wasn't."

"How can you be so sure?"

"I can tell by the cardboard and glue. They use better cardboard and glue in China."

"Jesus *fuckin'* Christ."

"Fact's a fact. Chinese box feels like a house."

"Look, all I want's a box that'll hold up for tonight. 'Case it comes down cats-and-dogs again."

"One I pick out is gonna last us a *week,*" Larry said, still rooting in the trash. "The reason bein' that those Chinamen make their boxes outta—"

He suddenly broke off, staring past Larry's shoulder.

Larry turned to see what had got him so damn interested.

The guy walking up to them was holding a badge in one hand and a drawing of some guy's face and upper body in the other.

"Detective Bayliss, Baltimore City Homicide," he said.

They watched him without response, Larry peering out over the side of the Dumpster, Jos standing inches away from him on the sidewalk.

"Either of you know the man in this sketch?" Bayliss asked, holding the composite out toward them. He'd been on his way over to Grant Street when he spotted the pair, and had figured it was worth stopping to ask a few questions.

They said nothing.

"Be good if somebody answered me," Bayliss said after a long moment.

They said nothing, their expressions completely neutral.

"I'm looking for some information," Bayliss said, trying not to get annoyed. "In connection with a shooting that took place yesterday."

They stuck to being silent.

"You fellas understand me?"

Blank stares.

Still holding out the picture in one hand, Bayliss tapped it with the pointer finger of the other.

"Here, see?" he said, mouthing the words slowly, going on the presumption they really *didn't* understand him. "This man. Name's Jake. The police are looking for him."

He waited. Took a deep breath. Waited a little longer.

Not a peep out of them.

This was proving to be a total waste of time.

"Listen," he said, making a final attempt at getting through to them. "All I want is to be pointed in the right direction. Whatever you tell me stays between us."

Nothing.

"Okay," Bayliss said, giving up in disgust. "Appreciate your cooperation."

He returned the sketch to his pocket, gave both of

them a bilious look, and strode away under their wall-eyed gazes.

Jos waited till he'd gone out of earshot, then turned back to Larry.

"You find us a box yet?" he asked. He figured the best way to get screwed was to talk to the cops, and had no intention of doing it. Not now, not later, not ever if he could help it.

Larry inspected a flattened box and tossed it aside. Made in the U.S.A.

"Gimme a chance," he huffed. "I only been at it a coupla minutes."

The Baltimore headquarters of Durham, Jellersen & Fisk was in an impressive Mt. Vernon townhouse with a curved, iron-railed stairway leading up from the ground floor reception/mailroom area to the traders' desks on the second floor and the executive offices on the third.

Erected in the early 1800s, the redbrick building had been designated a historical landmark soon after its purchase by the brokerage firm two years ago, William Durham was explaining to Munch from across his enormous desk.

"That sort of cuts both ways. Looks good on a prospectus, but makes it difficult for us to fix up the place," he said. "I can't hang a photo of my wife and kids on the wall without a permit from the Maryland Historical Society."

Munch tried to look sympathetic but didn't figure his performance would win him any acting awards.

Give him a chance to spend his workdays in the lavish comfort of an office like Durham's and he'd gladly deal with a hundred supervisory committees.

The place oozed money. The brick fireplace that dominated the room had moldings and pilasters of some light buff wood and a painted overmantel view of a nineteenth-century sailing fleet in the Port of Baltimore. A pair of smaller decorative panels, one on each side of the doorway, showed similar waterfront scenes. The lamp, paper rack, pen tray, blotter ends, calender, inkstand, and letter opener on Durham's desk were made of heavy cast bronze and looked as if they'd come from a pricey antique showroom.

"Sir," Munch said, "if I may, I'd like to talk to you about Donna Anne MacIntyre."

"So I assumed when my secretary announced you were here to see me," Durham said, and shook his head regretfully. "It truly hasn't sunk in that she's gone. What happened to her is so hard to believe." He sighed. "Thank God there are people like you hunting down the killer."

Munch refrained from patting himself on the back.

"I saw the sketch of the man that did it in today's *Sun*. It's ghastly. The crazies seem to be everywhere you turn these days," Durham said. He picked up the paper knife and lightly tapped the flat of its blade against his blotter. "But I shouldn't waste your time, Detective. What do you want to know?"

Munch looked at him. Durham was a fleshy, pink-cheeked man of about fifty in a conservative pinstriped suit and gold-rimmed bifocals. His teeth were beauti-

fully even and white. His fingernails were professionally manicured. He wore a gold Rolex wristwatch.

Money.

"Why don't you start by telling me a little bit about
Donna," Munch said. "What she did here at your firm,
how she got along with her coworkers, whether she'd
been having any problems you might've been aware
of . . . anything that comes to mind."

Durham's face became confused. "Is all that really
important right now? I mean, if Donna was the victim
of a random shooting . . . ?"

"Sir, these are the kinds of things we ask in nearly
every case. As a matter of procedure."

Durham was still fidgeting with the paper knife.
Tap-tap.

"Yes, of course, forgive me. As you can imagine,
I'm quite upset," he said, and paused a beat. "Donna
was an outstanding individual. Intelligent, creative,
and industrious, yet absolutely honest."

Which, Munch thought, was a description that
sounded like it belonged on the astrological place mat
he'd gotten with his Chinese take-out the other night.

"What specifically was her job in the company?" he
asked. "Just so I'm clear on it."

"It would take hours to cite all her contributions to
our success," Durham said. "Donna originally worked
for me in the equity trading division of Goldman
Sachs. This was about five years ago, in New York.
When I left Goldman to launch this firm, I asked her
to join me as chief portfolio manager in the Baltimore-
D.C. office."

"Quite a move," Munch said.

"Both physically and in terms of her career," Durham said, nodding. "Donna was a native New Yorker. On the other hand, I'm Kent County going back five generations and had been anxious to get closer to my roots. Donna knew she'd have to make some adjustments, but frankly my offer was too good to pass up."

"How'd she like it once she got here?"

Durham shrugged a little. "I've heard Baltimore described as a sleepy southern hamlet that wants more than anything to be a world-class city, and in many ways it is precisely that. Half cosmopolitan, half white-trash trailer court. Donna missed the northern lights, so to speak. But she found her career very fulfilling, and I don't think she ever regretted her decision."

"Donna's sister told me she was credited with making a lot of money for your company," Munch said.

"And for our clients," Durham said. "Have you read the *Trendsetter* article?"

"Not yet," Munch said. "I've got a copy of it, though."

"A tremendous piece, and completely accurate. It will tell you about Donna's professional accomplishments in far more detail than I can right now."

"When was she promoted to vice president?"

"Three, four months ago," Durham said. "We were branching off into international markets and chose her to head the new division. She'd been developing programs that would bring our investors to foreign financial centers."

Munch was quiet a moment, then said, "Mr. Durham, could Donna have made any enemies as a result of her promotion? A jealous coworker, for example. Or someone who might've been competing for the same position and felt slighted when she was picked."

Durham seemed unhappy about the question. He raised his eyebrows and tapped his letter opener on the desk.

"Not that I know of," he said. "She was very fair with others. Decent. And people respected her for that."

"What about clients for whom she might have made losing investments? Nobody's batting average is perfect."

Durham gave him a wan smile.

"The magazine article really would explain a great deal about our firm," he said. "Donna's responsibilities no longer included handling individual portfolios. Furthermore, we are what's known in the business as a carriage trade house. Are you familiar with the term?"

Munch shook his head. If Durham was trying to make him feel like an ignorant plebian, he was doing a pretty good job.

"It means, in essence, that we gear our services to customers who can absorb even a considerable financial loss. New accounts are generally opened through the recommendation of past or present clients. We are very select."

"Deep pockets only, in other words," Munch said. Zing.

Durham put down the letter opener and crossed his arms.

"I suppose you could put it that way," he said.

The room was silent again. After about a minute Munch rose and buttoned his coat.

"I appreciate your cooperation, sir. This must be a very bad time."

Durham drew in a breath, let it out, nodded.

"Give me a call if you think of anything that seems important," Munch said.

"Yes, certainly. I want to do whatever I can to help. And likewise hope you'll keep me abreast of your progress," Durham said. He came around the desk and showed him to the door. "Why don't you leave your phone number with my secretary, Patricia?"

Munch told him he would, and left.

"Here," he said, handing Patricia his card on the way past her desk. "That's me."

A good-looking brunette with sapphire eyes and a pleasingly snug white sweater, she studied it in silence.

"No kidding, it really *is* me," he said.

She looked at the card another moment, her face serious. Then she slid open a desk drawer and put it away, still not answering him.

"So much for approach number three-seventy-seven," he said as he started toward the winding stairs.

The next-to-last stop on Pembleton's list was a homeless drop-in center on Barlowe Street, and the director of patient services there, a middle-aged woman with tired features named Sheila Stearns, seemed no more pleased to see him than Father Donnelly—or any of the other program administrators he'd interviewed that afternoon—had been.

"I don't recognize him," she said after glancing quickly at the workup of the suspect. "And I doubt he's ever been to our clinic."

"Why's that?" Pembleton asked.

"There are several reasons," she said. "Would you like me to go through all of them?"

He rubbed a hand across his shaved head.

"How about you start with a few."

"The vast majority of our patients are women and children who have been referred by someone at a shelter—usually a trained social worker," she said. "They arrive here in busses that are provided at our expense. No one gets through the door without a signed referral slip, and loitering outside the premises is strongly discouraged. These practices were worked out before we first opened, and show our sensitivity to the concerns of area residents, many of whom were afraid we'd be bringing deviants to their streets and schoolyards. They guarantee that no one with a history of drug addiction, violent behavior, or, unfortunately, some poor soul without a recommendation who has nowhere else to go, will receive attention at this center."

"And what sort of attention is that, exactly?"

"Upon arrival our patients are examined by a physician, treated for minor medical and hygienic problems, and then given some fresh clothing, food money, and a good night's sleep. This is a short-stay facility."

"Meaning?"

"The maximum period that a single patient or family group may remain here is a week."

"And nothing's ever happened? No incidents of a disruptive nature, that is?"

"Not in two years of operation." She looked across her desk at him. "We take our commitments and responsibilities very seriously, Detective."

Pembleton paused before he spoke. "Ma'am, I don't see how anything you've said rules out the possibility that the man we're looking for was admitted here in the past. He may have been a model patient at the time and subsequently become unstable. Or he could've known how to act like the rest of us whenever he was being observed by a doctor. Or just slipped through a crack in the system. If you'd provide me with access to your files—"

"I'm sorry, but that's out of the question. Given the problems we have with understaffing, it would make it impossible to perform our daily tasks. Moreover, there are issues of doctor-patient confidentiality. Our clinicians are physicians, licensed therapists, and so on. It may come as a surprise to you, but even the homeless are entitled to their civil rights."

"I could apply for a search warrant and have a judge sort out just what those rights are in this instance," Pembleton said.

"And I can pick up my phone and be talking to an

ACLU attorney in a flash," she said with tightly controlled anger. "I'm sure there are plenty of them who'd be willing to argue our position in court."

They sat there studying each other in silence.

"I don't understand," Pembleton said after a while. He was shaking his head. "I've been to half a dozen facilities like this today. Looking for information about a murder suspect, someone who may have gunned down a woman in cold blood. And I've hit a stone wall everywhere."

Stearns met his gaze again, held it an instant. Then she sat back in her chair, sighing, her attitude softening a little.

"Look," she said, "I don't mean to be intransigent, Detective. But there are people who would blame innocent mothers, many of whom are on the street because they have fled abusive environments, for the destructive act of a single man."

"So I've been told at least a dozen times," Pembleton said. "It's ridiculous."

"It is also reality. The two often go together, I think."

Pembleton produced a brief, strained laugh.

"The victim of the shooting had a name. Her life mattered. It had value."

"As do those of the twenty or thirty victims I help every day. And, if you'll forgive me for putting it bluntly, they are *still* alive and coping with this world, which to my way of looking at things gives them priority over a single dead woman."

"The needs of the many outweigh the needs of the few," Pembleton said.

A faint smile touched her lips.

"Something like that," she said. "Mr. Spock in *The Wrath of Khan,* isn't it?"

"Actually, Voltaire pretty much said it first," he said.

Sometimes, working a case, you caught a lucky break, although Bayliss believed you had to stick with every lead and keep your eyes wide open in order to be ready when it came your way. In a sense he likened it to playing the outfield in a baseball game. If you were picking lint out of your briefs when the flyball came sailing in your direction, you were either going to fumble, or, worse than that, miss the play altogether. You had to be ready.

Such were his thoughts as he approached the glass-walled indoor plaza, or mall, or pocket park, or whatever it was called and, glancing in from the street, saw the young black guy with the ratty, too-small quilted jacket and the scar, or ink spot, or keloid, or whatever the hell *it* was called on his cheek, sitting alone at one of the tables around the central water fountain, looking glazed and wired. Surrounding his legs was a collection of shopping bags that, as far as Bayliss could tell, were filled with soiled rags and little else. He quickened his pace, rounded the corner toward the entrance, and approached him.

"Hey, Ossie! Good to see you, man," he said, pulling up short of the circle of bags.

The guy sat there looking obliterated. His eyes were veined with red and deeply recessed in their sockets. There were ugly sores on his lips. He smelled bad.

"Mmm," he said.

Bayliss rotated his head, working a kink out of his neck, and suddenly realized he was alone except for Ossie and a sprinkling of other disheveled types slouched here and there at the picnic-style tables. It occurred to him that these enclosed public spaces might have seemed like a great idea in theory, and he supposed they looked magnificent when presented as scale miniatures in planning rooms across America, but it seemed unfathomable that the architects who sold them as year-round islands of calm for frazzled office workers had overlooked the probability— the *certainty*, even—that those workers would eventually be scared off by the ranks of homeless humanity wandering every urban landscape, people who weren't seeking lunch-hour respites from difficult jobs and prickly bosses, but rather from the sidewalks, alleys, vacant lots, and underground tunnels where they otherwise drifted through their existences. Dump them on the street and tell them to sink or swim, and what the hell did anybody expect, they'd bathe in rosewater and read up on their Emily Post?

"Listen to me, Ossie," Bayliss said. "That's your name, right? Ossie?"

The kid nodded his head slowly up and down.

"Okay, we're connecting here, and that's good," Bayliss said. He reached into his coat for the sketch he'd been showing around and held it up to Ossie's face. "See, Ossie, what I want you to do is take a look at the picture and tell me if it resembles anybody you know."

Ossie stared at the sketch without response.

"C'mon, buddy, I'm counting on you," Bayliss said.

The kid stared at the sketch.

"Steve," he said at last, barely opening his mouth to get out the word.

"Huh?"

"Thass Steve," Ossie said.

Bayliss looked at him. *"Steve?"*

The kid nodded.

"Not Jake."

The kid shook his head.

"Not Rich."

The kid shook his head.

"Steve."

"Is wha' he call hisself to me," the kid mumbled, nodding.

Which, Bayliss thought, could mean that three different men had been separately identified as the one in the sketch; or that the *same* man was using three different names; or that *two* men had been identified, one of them using a single name and the other using two names.

"This guy Steve a friend of yours?" he asked.

Ossie merely shrugged.

"You want to explain what that means?"

"Man hang out wi' me sometime," Ossie said, and shrugged again.

85

"He ever mention anything to you about having been in Vietnam?" Bayliss asked.

"Always talkin' 'bout how he fight inna fuckin' desert," Ossie said.

Bayliss looked at him. "The Gulf War, you mean?"

"Yeah."

Which, Bayliss thought, tended to support the single man—three names hypothesis. While anything was possible, it was pretty easy to believe that a guy who'd make up several different aliases for himself would also make up several different versions of his military background, and it was a little harder to believe that two different homeless men, both of whom coincidentally fit the artist's profile of the murder suspect, also coincidentally would be veterans of separate wars, and, by further coincidence, get off on telling stories about their battlefield exploits. But how did it all bear upon the two man—three name scenario?

The whole thing was making his head spin.

"All right, Ossie, I've got one more simple question," he said. "Where can I find your boy Steve?"

Ossie sat very still, seemingly back in the Twilight Zone.

"Tell me where I can find him," Bayliss repeated.

Ossie kept staring his abstracted stare.

Bayliss put the picture away and leaned forward so their faces were close together. It was something he'd rather not have done; the stench coming off the kid was overwhelming.

"Ossie, I'm a cop, you gotta know that by now," he said, trying not to gag. "And you also gotta know that anybody who gets a look at your highbeams can see you've been sucking on a crack pipe."

He paused, giving that a chance to penetrate.

The kid stared.

"Ossie, I sure hope you're not putting me on with the zombie routine," Bayliss said, "because unless you give me an answer, I'm gonna toss all the crap out of your bags and kick it around the floor here until I find something illegal. I'd only need a few crumbs to lock you up. Or maybe an empty vial. Or your stem."

Ossie swallowed, his lips moving slightly.

"What's it gonna be?" Bayliss said.

Ossie took another swallow. A long one.

Finally his eyes met Bayliss's.

"You lookin' for that crazy man, check out th' shelter on Alan Street tonight," he said.

"You sure?"

"Yeah. We been crashin' there the past couple weeks."

Bayliss stood up straight and smiled.

He'd gotten his lucky break, all right, and was thinking it just might be the start of a winning roll.

FIVE

IN BALTIMORE, AS in New York, Boston, Washington, Los Angeles, and scores of other cities across this fair land of hope and opportunity, the principles upon which the system of public homeless shelters operates are simple: pack as many individuals as possible into the largest space you can find, assign each of them a lumpy metal bed and clothing locker for what is generally an overnight stay and—here's where the hope and opportunity come into play, so listen up, class—*hope* none of them, or at least manageably few of them, will take advantage of the *opportunity* to croak from a drug overdose in the bathroom or to rob, assault, or murder the poor slob lying asleep on the next cot over.

Simple, boys and girls.

For over a hundred years after its construction during the Civil War, the large brick building that presently housed the Alan Street Shelter had served as an armory for various branches of the U.S. military. However, come the 1980s, Ron and Nancy, the end of the Cold War, and joyous prosperity for a miniscule fraction of our country's citizens, come this magnificent flourishing of hope and opportunity for those with plenty to invest in real estate, CMOs, and junk bonds, and the need for large reserves of arms and equipment became less pressing than the need for places to cram the growing number of poor people whom Nan and the Gipper, may our memories of them endure, hadn't invited to the party. And so, many of the aging structures were emptied of their obsolete rifles and ammunition, mothballed combat fatigues, forty-year-old C rations, and whatever else had been stashed away in them (all of which was either trashed or hauled off by the truckload to other existing stockpiles), and then converted into crude facilities for the homeless, as was the case here on Alan Street.

The moment Bayliss entered the place he felt like reeling from the smell that assaulted him. Likewise for Pembleton and Munch, who had walked in at his side. The air, if you could call it that, stank of piss, excrement, and other bodily discharges none of them wanted to think about. It stank of sickness and empty stomachs. It stank of despair in all its terrible, abounding forms.

"Jesus," Bayliss said, clapping his hand over his nose and mouth.

"What's wrong, Timmy, got no odor-eaters up your sleeve?" Munch said.

"What d'you mean?"

"I mean why stick with the standard magic tricks, when with a little hocus-pocus this place could be spanking clean. You can bet it's where *I'd* want to come looking for help."

Bayliss glared at him, his hand still covering the lower half of his face. Was there anything Munch wouldn't joke about?

"You get use'ta it after a while," said the uniformed guard behind the sign-in desk near the door.

All three detectives turned their attention to him at once.

"You guys cops?"

"Yeah," Pembleton said, flashing his tin.

"Mystery solved." The guard scratched a pouchy cheek. "Anyway, like I was saying, you get use'ta the stink."

"That so?"

"Sure. The nose goes dead. Same as my taste buds did after a few years of my wife's cookin'." The guard chuckled.

"Uh-huh," Pembleton said. He slapped the comp of the wanted man onto the desk. "Sir—"

"Lost parta my hearin', too. *Before* I got married. Lived in this apartment next door to a firehouse. Sirens goin' off night and day," the guard said. He pointed to his right ear, ignoring the sketch. "That's the bad one. On account I mostly sleep on my left side, and the pillow stopped the noise from gettin' that ear."

"Another of nature's fascinating adaptations," Munch said.

The guard chuckled again, really getting on Pembleton's nerves now.

"Sir, could you please take a look at the sketch and tell me if it looks like any of the people who've been staying here recently?" he said, making the time-out sign with his hands.

The guard glanced down at it.

"You gotta be kidding," he said, and laughed yet again, his funnybone obviously tickled by a whole range of comedic approaches.

"What is it?"

"What it is, is that your picture could be of three-quarters of the guys who come here every night. Forget about me not bein' able to smell, it's a wonder my *eyes* don't fall out, considering how many faces like this I gotta look at." The guard cocked a thumb over his shoulder. "Take a gander an' you'll see what I mean."

Pembleton did. The immense room—or ward, as it almost could have been considered—was filled front to rear with some hundred and fifty beds lined up in more or less even rows, and even though there was only a scattering of occupants at this relatively early hour of nine P.M., a good portion, if not actually three-quarters, of the ragged, bearded, stocking-capped men shuffling between the sleeping area and the partitioned-off soup kitchen in back did indeed resemble the artist's depiction to varying degrees.

"An' if you think *that's* confusin', wait'll the rest of 'em come in from beggin' at eleven, twelve o'clock," the guard said.

Pembleton frowned and reached for his sketch. "The guy we're after has been seen wearing a green army coat. He sometimes rants and raves about having gotten wounded in Vietnam."

"Which cuts the possibilities to maybe thirty or forty average pains in my ass."

Pembleton's frown deepened.

"He also sometimes goes by the name of Jake," he said.

"Or Rich," Munch said.

"Or Steve," Bayliss said through his fingers.

The guard quickly straightened up in his chair.

"God damn," he said. "I know him. He's here right now."

The detectives traded glances with each other, Bayliss's hand dropping from his face now, all three of them feeling the little jolt every cop felt inside before making a collar.

"Where?"

"There," the guard said, turning in his chair to point. "Putting away his I'm-a-crippled-vet sign."

Pembleton's eyes followed the trajectory of his finger, came to rest on a man who was standing over by the lockers along the room's right wall, his back turned, his locker's open door hiding most of his face from view.

Still, Pembleton could see enough to make his heart beat very loudly in his ears, drowning out the general clatter of the room: an army coat, wool hat, and long, stringy brown hair.

"Guy's crazy as shit, got a new name for every day

of the week," the guard said. "Jake was yesterday. Today it's Seth."

"We have to talk to him."

"The administrator's out getting something to eat. I should really make you wait till she comes back before you do that."

"C'mon, give us a break," Bayliss said. "This nut blew open a woman's head."

The guard didn't say anything for a minute. Then he grunted and looked straight down at the registration book on his desk.

"Go ahead," he said. "I can't see you."

They strode past his desk and hurried toward the back of the vaulted room, Pembleton moving along the row of lockers, Munch and Bayliss weaving between the beds on his left, spreading out so they could block his way to the door if he decided to take off running.

"Sir," Pembleton said, coming up behind the guy, "if you've got a minute, I'd like to ask you a few questions."

The guy pulled his head out of the locker and turned around. One of his hands was on the locker door. The other hung loosely at his side.

Pembleton stood where he could see them.

"I'm with the police," he said. "Please step away from the locker."

The guy glanced left, then right, his face tense, looking at Pembleton out of the corners of his eyes.

Pembleton kept watching the man's hands, kept them in sight in case he tried to make a grab for a gun.

"Step away from the locker," he repeated in a firm voice.

The guy stopped turning his head from side to side and regarded him. His cheeks were thin and oily above his beard and there was a bright, edgy gleam in his eyes.

A moment passed.

Another.

Pembleton watched his hands.

The guy's mouth suddenly dropped wide open.

"Incoming!" he yelled at the top of his lungs, slamming the locker door shut with an explosive crash that made everyone in the room turn their eyes in his direction. *"INNCOMMMING!"*

And the next thing Pembleton knew, the guy was diving past him with his hands covering his head as if mortar rounds were about to come falling from the sky. He dropped to the floor, slid on his belly for a couple of feet, sprang briefly up onto his haunches, and then tucked-and-rolled into the middle of the ward as if he were no longer in contemporary Baltimore, U.S.A., land of hope and opportunity, but had been flung backward through time and space into a steaming Vietnamese jungle. Behind Pembleton, his fellow detectives had not yet recovered from their startlement as the suspect came bowling into the narrow gap between their legs, staggering Munch to one side, and knocking Bayliss flat on his bottom.

Then, bouncing back to his feet, the guy took off running.

Throughout the entire room, meanwhile, guards as

well as residents were scattering every which way, screaming and shouting, dropping trays of soup and bread, jumping under beds and cafeteria tables, and tripping all over each other in a mad panic, presumably seeking cover from the surprise attack that Jake, Steve, Rich, Seth, or whoever he was, had fearfully warned was being launched at the shelter from some nearby NVA stronghold.

Realizing in a blink that he'd be unable to fire his gun in the thick of those scrambling, ducking bodies, Pembleton went dashing after the wanted man, hurtling between Munch and Bayliss, bounding over a tangle of arms and legs, faltering briefly as a wild-eyed guy cut unknowingly in front of him, pushing a bed across his path as if it were a hospital gurney, probably convinced he was rushing through elephant grass to bring the wounded aboard evac choppers. Pembleton detoured around the bed, saw the wanted man turn toward the door and rushed to catch up, plowing through the stampeding, awful-smelling crowd, gaining, gaining, then driving himself toward the fleeing suspect in a final, breathless sprint, throwing his arms around his waist and tackling him to the floor an instant before he would have reached the street.

They wrestled there inside the entrance, Pembleton digging his knee into the small of the guy's back, pinning him down on his stomach as he continued screaming and thrashing like a man on a torturer's rack. Twisting his arm behind his back with one hand, Pembleton reached for his cuffs with the other, fumbling them off his belt, getting out the cuffs only to have them go flying from his grasp as the guy suddenly reared like a wild stallion and almost threw him off his perch.

Pembleton was struggling mightily to hang on when someone came racing up from behind him, knelt to pick up the cuffs, grabbed the guy's left hand, grabbed his right hand, and quickly slapped on the bracelets.

Pembleton expelled a sigh of relief, craned his head around, and found himself looking into the big, jowly face of the guard from the sign-in desk.

"You better put the sonuvabitch under arrest," the guard said, beaming back at him.

For Frank Pembleton, all roads led to the Box. This cramped, windowless, brick-walled interview room on the second floor of headquarters was where he got his payoff for the hard work that was put into a case, regardless of what happened after it was passed on to the theater of the absurd known as a criminal trial. Where he relentlessly probed and confronted the worst part of human nature, recognizing that the thoughts running through the minds of killers were dark reflections of his own, and turning the darkness against itself to extract the truth, and hopefully a confession, from the encounter. The ease with which he could get into the head of a suspect was unnerving even to other seasoned murder cops. It was also, they acknowledged, the key to why he had closed more cases than anyone on the squad.

At 10:05 on Wednesday night, just over twenty-seven hours after Donna Anne MacIntyre was gunned to death while walking her dog, the homeless man suspected of having committed the crime was booked into custody, photographed, fingerprinted, and then brought into the Box, where he was seated at a table and once again advised of his right to an attorney and his right to remain silent under *Miranda*. An assistant district attorney named Paul Tessier arrived to observe the interrogation at 11:30, with counsel from the public defender's office, Deborah Reeves, showing up on behalf of the suspect a few minutes before midnight. Also present were police videographer J. H. Brodie and a stenographer named Joyce Chin.

Barely seven minutes into Thursday morning, lead detective Pembleton and his partner on the MacIntyre investigation, Tim Bayliss, began their questioning.

"Sir, do you know why we've brought you here?" Pembleton said, wanting to establish for the record that the suspect was neither disoriented nor mentally incapable of understanding his rights.

The guy sat there with his head bowed, slumped forward in his chair, holding his watchcap on the table in front of him, his fingers kneading and tugging at the watchcap. He was still wearing his army coat despite the warmth and closeness of the room.

"You think I killed that lady," he said after a long moment, his voice low and raspy.

"Did you?"

He shook his head without raising his eyes. "All I know is what I heard on the street."

"Such as?"

"She got shot over on Hester, and you guys've been asking questions, showing around a picture that looks kind of like me. I saw it on the front of the paper."

"It really *does* resemble you, doesn't it?"

The guy just shrugged.

"So you knew the police were looking for you, but chose not to come in and talk to us," Pembleton said, pressing him a little.

"Right."

"Even though you had nothing to do with killing Donna Anne MacIntyre?"

"Right."

"So why not try and clear this mess up?"

He shrugged again.

"Wouldn't that make sense if you're telling the truth about being innocent?"

"I don't know the lady. Don't know anything about her. And I didn't kill nobody."

"Which brings me right back to wondering why you haven't tried to contact us. And why you ran when we found you at the shelter."

"I wasn't running."

"Oh no?"

"No."

"Well, I know there was also some sliding and tumbling involved, but, that little technicality aside, what else would you call it?"

"I was confused. Thought for a minute I was back in the Big V. It happens sometimes when I got strains."

"What kind of strains?"

"Strains like knowing the cops are after my ass."

"So you're saying you had, what, some kind of flashback?"

The guy nodded. "If any of you'd ever been through a shelling, I wouldn't have to explain."

Pembleton looked at him skeptically.

"While we're on the subject," he said, "you mind telling me what outfit you were with in the war?"

"It was Special Forces. A White Star unit. Did three tours, operated out of a secret base near the Laotian border."

"Keep going."

"Most of this is still classified. I took an oath."

"Just tell me what you can."

"We worked in four-man teams. Those guys were like family and they're all dead except me. Sometimes our mission was S&D."

"That's search and destroy?"

"Yeah. We'd go out on random contact patrol, seek out targets, what they used to call frontier sealing. Or crawl into spider holes and clean the bastards out. A few times we crossed the border to liberate high-level POWs. I can't talk about the rest of the missions. Once they dropped us in the boonies we were on our own. And we did what we had to do. I loved those guys, man."

"I assume your service record can be verified?" asked Pembleton, thinking all this sounded like the plot of a bad paperback novel he'd read, to his lasting regret.

The guy shook his head. "It was spookwar. Never happened, you know what I mean."

"So you're saying there's no *proof* of your story—"

"Detective," Reeves said, "I really can't see how my client's experiences in Vietnam have any bearing on your investigation."

"Until you decide to make posttraumatic shock disorder part of his defense," Pembleton said. "But maybe I shouldn't be giving you ideas."

She stared at him icily.

Pembleton grinned at her, then tossed Bayliss a look that meant he wanted him to move in along a different track.

"Maybe we should back up a second," Bayliss said, and approached the table from where he'd been leaning against the observation window. "I mean, it would be nice if you could give us your real name before we take this any further, don't you think?"

"I already did."

"No," Bayliss said. "See, what you gave us is *one* of the names you use. Seth Wilkins, according to what you told the desk sergeant who booked you."

"There a problem with that?"

"No, no, I think it's a good name. It's just, you know, that some friends of yours told us—"

"I got no friends."

"Well, some *acquaintances* said you also call yourself Rich. And Jake."

"And Steve, lest we forget," Pembleton said.

"Rich, Jake, and Steve," Bayliss said. "Besides Seth, of course."

"So what of it?"

Bayliss tried to curb his sarcasm. "Well, part of our job is to establish your identity, so we can either include you or exclude you as someone who might've had a motive to commit the crime. If you're not guilty of anything, it'll help us prove—"

"They were my buddies in the war, okay?" the guy interrupted, agitatedly crushing his hat into a ball. "Just before Tet in sixty-eight we were in this enemy compound, and things went wrong, and there was nobody to pull us out, and I lost 'em. I lost 'em, man. So once in a while I use their names. Makes me feel better about being alive."

"Okay, now we're making progress. I'm glad we got that straightened out," Bayliss said, thinking the guy sounded like a character out of a Chuck Norris flick he'd once watched on cable and was forever wishing he hadn't.

He gave Pembleton a look not unlike the one Pembleton had given him a few minutes before.

"Seth," Pembleton picked up. "Uh, it's okay if I call you Seth, isn't it?"

"Yeah."

"Because if it isn't, I can call you Harvey, or Caesar, or Mr. Mxyztplk, or any bogus handle you prefer."

"That's uncalled for, Detective. Mr. Wilkins is being very cooperative, and he's already explained—"

Pembleton held up his hand to stop her.

"Point taken," he said, flashing a grin at her again.

"I don't want anyone to think I lack respect for our combat veterans." He turned back to the suspect. "Seth, we all want to get to the truth here. So tell me, where were you last night between six-thirty and seven o'clock?"

Seth looked up at him for the first time.

"Getting something to eat," he said, briefly making eye contact.

"Where?"

"At the St. Ignatius soup kitchen. Down in the parish hall."

"You sure about that?"

"Yeah."

"Why didn't you eat at the shelter?"

"The place is a shithole. Everything about it stinks, the food most of all. I won't touch it."

"Uh-huh," Pembleton said, and paused. "The reason I ask about the church is that maybe the priest there, Father Kelly—"

"His name's Donnelly," Seth said.

Which Pembleton had, of course, known.

"Right, my mistake. But what I was saying was that if Father *Donnelly*—whom I spoke to yesterday, by the way—would confirm you were at the church when the shooting took place, we'd know this whole thing's been a mix-up. Isn't that so?"

"I guess." Seth had gone back to staring down at his cap.

"Our only problem's that when he saw the drawing of the suspect, which you've admitted looks a lot like you—"

"My client said nothing of the sort—"

"Which *many* of us think bears a great resemblance to you," Pembleton said. "When I showed Father Donnelly our drawing, he said he didn't recognize you."

"Perhaps because the composite really doesn't look like Mr. Wilkins, supporting his claim that he isn't the same man who was identified by your eyewitnesses," Reeves said.

"Or because he's never been *at* that soup kitchen before," Pembleton said.

"Score one for each of us."

Pembleton sighed and turned to the suspect.

"Look, all I'm trying to do is find out whether you have some way of verifying that you were at St. Ignatius's yesterday," he said.

"Don't know how many times you want me to tell you, I was. But there's got to have been two hundred other people like me there, too. And Father Donnelly's always doing things. Taking care of business. Most nights you hardly notice him around."

"What about those two hundred people you mentioned? Did any of *them* see you?"

"I don't know. I keep to myself."

"What about the volunteers? There must be folks who prepare and serve the food, dishwashers—"

"I don't know."

"How long did you stay at the church?" Bayliss asked.

"I'm not sure. The place closes up at eight. I was out before that."

"Before eight o'clock."

"Yeah."

"Then where'd you head?"

"To the shelter."

"*Straight* to the shelter?" Pembleton asked.

"Yeah."

"And how long did it take you to get there?"

"I don't remember, maybe twenty minutes. . . ."

"So you would've signed in before eight-thirty?"

"I guess."

"Well, that's okay, we'll be able to check the registration book for the exact time."

No answer.

Pembleton braced his elbows on the table and leaned forward until his left cheek was almost brushing against the suspect's right one.

"Just out of curiosity, Seth, am I making you nervous? Because you seem a little tense," he said in a hushed voice.

Seth hesitated, then nodded slowly in reply.

"Thought so, from the way you're sort of wringing that cap in your hands. And how you keep staring down at it when you answer my questions instead of looking into my eyes. It gives the impression you're hiding something. Maybe feeling guilty."

"I ain't."

"The block where Donna Anne was killed, don't you hang around there looking for handouts?"

"Sometimes."

"Were you there Tuesday?"

"No."

"Not at all?"

"I don't know. Could've been early on, I move around a lot. But at six-thirty I was getting my supper."

"Seth, listen to me." Pembleton dropped his voice to a near whisper. "We have a half dozen witnesses who saw you walk up to that woman and blow her head apart. Almost every one of those people has seen you before, read your sign, heard your war stories. Some of them have given you spare change."

"So what of it?"

"So they've looked at your face up close. And they'll be able to recognize you if we bring them in to make an identification."

"It wasn't me who shot her."

"You can say that. You can keep denying things. But don't tell me you never saw her on the street before, maybe on her way home from work, maybe walking the dog like she was last night. Shopping for gourmet olives and French pastries while you're out begging for quarters. Young, sexy, expensive clothes, money written all over her. Looking the other way when she passed you. Pretending not to notice you. Or dropping a quarter in your hand just to get you out of her face, when you knew she had so much more in her wallet, so much more to throw around. . . ."

"Detective Pembleton," Reeves said, "we're trying to comply with you in every way. But if you keep speaking in a tone I can't hear, I'm going to advise my client to break this off."

"Seth, please," Pembleton said, ignoring her. "It doesn't pay to keep lying. The eyewitness testimony

106

alone is enough to convict you. You'll feel better if you explain what happened. If you help me understand why you snapped—"

Reeves rose angrily off her chair. "Detective, I won't give you another warning."

Pembleton looked at her, drew in a breath, and sat back.

There was a long silence in the room.

"Gentlemen, it's way past the witching hour, and everybody's nerves are shot," Reeves said, her tone calmer now. "Can we agree it's time to call it a night?"

More silence.

Pembleton and Bayliss exchanged looks.

At last Pembleton turned to Reeves, sighed tiredly, and nodded.

"Sleep well, Counselor," he said, rising from his chair. "I'll see you tomorrow at the lineup."

"So what do you think?" Bayliss asked.

"That we've got a lot of work to do before there's any kind of case against our rogue warrior," Pembleton said.

They were standing outside the interview room admiring Deborah Reeves's proportions as she strode toward the elevators in her slingbacks.

Bayliss uncoupled his eyes from the back of her skirt and faced Pembleton. "You're kidding me, right?"

"No," he said plainly, glancing at his wristwatch. "My sense of humor goes to bed after 1 A.M."

"Frank, we've got all those witnesses. You said yourself in the Box that—"

"We've got five people who heard gunshots, looked in their direction, and spotted someone who resembles our suspect fleeing the scene. Not one of them actually saw Seth Wilkins—assuming that's his real name—walk up to Donna and pull the trigger."

"*Come on,* Frank. The details you're leaving out are that most of the witnesses also saw a gun in his hand and that nobody except Wilkins was near the victim."

"Or someone who looked like Wilkins. You heard the guard at the shelter say our sketch resembled half the guys that sign in at his desk. Plus it was a dark, wet night," Pembleton said. "Eyes can be decieved, as you ought to know, Houdini."

Bayliss ignored the last comment.

"What about the gun?" he asked.

"We don't *have* any gun. And even if we did, there's nothing at this point that would connect it—or, for that matter, any *other* firearm to Wilkins."

"We can have his skin and clothing tested for gunpowder residue—"

"And I doubt the findings will do us any good. This guy may be nuts, but he doesn't seem stupid. Assuming he's the killer, he could've found a sink and scrubbed himself afterward. And given the small size of the gun, and the fact that the shooting took place outdoors, it's iffy whether chemical trace analysis will turn up anything conclusive." Pembleton yawned and stretched. "At this hour, I won't *touch* the issue of motive, or the very big question of how a homeless beggar would come to own a PPK, which is essentially a collector's gun that costs maybe six, seven hundred dollars. *If* you can find one in a shop."

Bayliss looked at him. "What the hell are you getting at, Frank? I mean, you really think we might have the wrong man?"

"I'm playing devil's advocate. And my point is that we'd better start tracking down all the info we can about Mr. Wilkins. Check out his name and alibi. Run his prints through AFIS and see whether he has a jacket—and if he does, whether any of the priors involve use of a gun. See if he's collecting any kind of veteran's compensation that would back up his tales of guts and glory—"

"Okay, Frank. Enough," Bayliss said crankily. "I know how to do my job."

"Who's saying you don't?" Pembleton said. "I'm only worried that unless every one of our witnesses IDs Wilkins as the shooter in the lineup, or some corroborative evidence turns up that supports our murder charge, the long, leggy, and very capable Ms. Reeves is going to have him out on the street within twelve hours."

They stood there in the empty corridor outside the squad room, neither of them speaking.

"All this, and you still haven't told me whether you honestly believe Wilkins could be innocent," Bayliss said after a while.

He waited for a response.

Waited some more.

"You're right, I haven't," Pembleton said finally, and walked off toward the coffee room without another word.

Identification Parade Form

Time in: ___10:00 a.m.___   Date: ___10/30/97___
Witness number: ___3___   Time out: ___10:20 a.m.___

Witness:
This is a lineup of __10__ people. Would you look them over carefully and, if you see any person or persons that you recognize as having participated in the offense or incident for which you are a witness, please point them out by numbering from left . . . (6)

Identification lineup held at the town of: ___Baltimore County___
Complainant's name: ___State of Maryland___

Date of occ.: ___10/28___   Occ. number: ___30764___

John Gage	#1 (from left)
Carlton Edwards	#2 (from left)
Andy Bennett	#3 (from left)
Gordon Tosswill	#4 (from left)
Mark Holzman	#5 (from left)
Seth Wilkins	#6 (from left)
Anthony Bates	#7 (from left)
Clyde Teel	#8 (from left)
Richard Porter	#9 (from left)
J. H. Brodie	#10 (from left)

Witness: _Betty Li Joong (sign)_   *Betty Li Joong*
Officer in charge of lineup: ___Det. Sgt. Kay Howard___
Remarks: _Witness recognized accused (Seth Wilkins) with certainty on two separate viewings. Accused nervous but made no attempt at altering appearance or voice._

Recording officer: <u>Frank Pembleton</u>
Officer in charge of witness upon exit: <u>PO Robert Hollis</u>
Security officers in lineup room: <u>PO Robert Hollis; PO Douglas Rollins</u>
Others inside lineup room: <u>Det. John Munch; L. Al Giardello; Paul Tessier (A.D.A., Baltimore County); Deborah Reeves (Public Defender, Baltimore County)</u>

"That makes a perfect three out of three, Counsel," Giardello said to Reeves. They, along with Tessier and the investigating detectives, were standing behind the two-way mirror in the viewing area beside the lineup room. "The suspect has been identified by Desmond Coates, Karim Hayes, and now Mrs. Joong."

"All that does is confirm what nobody's even arguing about," she said. "My client's a panhandler whose preferred foraging ground is Hester Street. As far as I can see, that's the only thing to which your witnesses will be able to testify with any credibility. You want to prosecute Mr. Wilkins for loitering, be my guest."

Pembleton fired Bayliss a glance that said *I told you so*.

"And where's your fourth witness, by the way?" Reeves asked.

"Mr. Kessler was in a meeting and couldn't be reached," Bayliss said. He was gazing into Deborah Reeves's lustrous blue eyes and thinking she looked sharp and magnificently assembled and not at all like someone who had only left the station at one-thirty that same morning. "We'll bring him down at a later time."

"I wouldn't bother, unless he's got more to offer than the others."

"Such as?" Pembleton said.

"Having actually seen my client *shoot* someone, for openers," she said.

Pembleton refrained from glancing at Bayliss again.

"These so-called witnesses aside, I've yet to hear a single good reason why Mr. Wilkins is having to suffer your allegations, let alone remain in a cell," Reeves went on. "Your high-tech fingerprint file didn't give you any hits. He's Ajax clean."

"Or his record is, anyway," Munch said.

"Hysterical," she said. "You ought to be doing stand-up."

"So I've been told," Munch said.

"Your client *has* spent long periods in psychiatric institutions over the past two decades," Tessier, the A.D.A., said to Reeves.

"And does anything in his case history suggest a pattern of violent behavior?"

Tessier sighed. Beanstalk thin, he was at six-foot-five the tallest person in the room, and his rounded shoulders reflected a lifelong self-consciousness about his height and frame.

"Deborah, the man was only brought in hours ago. You know as well as I do that we haven't had time to get copies of his records," he said.

She shrugged. "The very fact that you were able to obtain any information at all about Mr. Wilkins demonstrates that he's been voluntarily cooperating with the detectives. He could've lied about his identity—"

Pembleton emitted a harsh burst of laughter. "*Co-*

operating? Just because he gave us his real name? That's ridiculous."

"Besides, the VA hasn't found anything so far to back up his claims of military service," Bayliss said.

Reeves shrugged again. "He *did* say he was part of a clandestine operation—"

"Oh come on," Pembleton said.

"Look, I don't even see a *prima facie* case here," she said. "You've got no murder weapon, no forensic evidence linking him to the crime, and no motive—or maybe we're to believe he mistook the victim for a booby-trapped Viet Cong."

"Sounds good to me."

"Let's bring this discussion back to where it should be, okay?" Giardello said. "Three people left this room within the past hour, each of whom independently made your client as the man they saw running from the body of Donna MacIntyre. With a gun in his hand, I might add."

"I won't go around in circles with you," Reeves said. "The only 'should be' in this situation involves your dismissing all charges against Mr. Wilkins in accordance with his Fourth Amendment rights. It may come as news, but the homeless and impoverished are entitled to the same constitutional protections as the rest of us."

"You've got to be kidding," Pembleton said. "None of this has anything to do with his social class—"

"We'll see whether Wayne Morley agrees," she interrupted, flashing a look at him.

Pembleton looked back at her.

"The homeless advocate?" he said.

"I talked to him this morning," she said. Her eyes remained locked on his. "We've arranged to meet."

"Deborah, be reasonable. Morley lives to see his face on the six o'clock news," Tessier said. "Let's not have this get out of hand—"

"It already *is* out of hand, and will continue to be until you give my client back his freedom," Reeves said curtly. "Since none of you seem inclined to do that, however, I don't think there's anything more for us to talk about."

And with that she picked up her briefcase and whisked out of the room, not bothering to shut the door behind her, leaving the rest of them momentarily speechless.

Finally Giardello turned to the others, scowling.

"Barnfather won't like this one damn bit," he said, and followed Reeves into the corridor.

SIX

"WAYNE MORLEY?" LEWIS said, tossing the football to Munch. "Ain't he the guy who led that hunger strike in Washington last year, slept out on the Lincoln Memorial all winter?"

Munch reached up and caught the ball as it came arcing over his desk.

"Actually, I think it was the Mall," he said. "Jerk'll do anything for attention, but you ask me he had a lunch box hidden under his coat."

"Aren't you guys being a little cynical?" Howard said. "I mean, it's one thing to want publicity for yourself, and it's another to want it for a cause you believe in."

"Get real, Kay. Name a line of sneakers Air Morleys and he'd die happy."

Munch fired the ball past her desk to Kellerman, making sure its flight path took it just beyond her reach.

He knew she wanted the ball and therefore he wouldn't throw it to her.

She knew he knew she wanted it and therefore she made no attempt to catch it.

This ongoing contest of wills had something of a long history.

The football had been in the squad room longer than any of the detectives assigned to Giardello's command, and in fact it had been there since those barbarous, dimly remembered days before the enlightened Age of Giardello. Worn smooth, half-deflated, its stitches loose and ratty, it was considered a sort of bedraggled yet tenacious mascot by everyone on the squad, who passed it around in moments of intense deliberation and idle conversation alike . . . everyone, that is, except Kay, who, to her great if unvoiced chagrin, had *not once* been thrown the ball in her half decade as a murder cop. There were three reasons for this—the first being that her fellows in the otherwise all-male squad, merry sexist pranksters that they were, had conspired not to toss it her way until she got visibly angry about being left out; the second being Howard's bristling awareness of this obvious conspiracy; and the third being her obstinate refusal to exhibit any visible sign that it had been angering her *to no end*.

Given the personalities involved, the stalemate seemed likely to continue into perpetuity.

"By the way, Brodie, you were a mean-looking bad guy in that lineup," Kellerman said, and bombed the football over to him.

"The whole thing being videotaped and all, I sort of considered it a walk-on," Brodie said, making his catch. "You know, like Hitchcock always did. And Scorcese in *Taxi Driver*. I even saw Barry Levinson do it on some cop show he produces for TV."

He lobbed the ball back across Kay's desk to Lewis, who quickly relayed it to Bayliss.

"You really think Reeves is gonna talk Morley into muckin' around in your case?" Lewis asked him.

"I dunno." Bayliss gave Pembleton a short overhand pass. "But she could talk *me* into anything."

"He'll bite," Pembleton declared stonily, and dropped the ball into his open desk drawer. "Mark my words, by tomorrow there'll be reporters crawling all over us."

The game of catch concluded, Munch picked up the thin pile of phone memos that had accumulated on his desk while he'd been watching the lineup. The first two calls he'd gotten were from A.D.A. Ed Danvers, the prosecutor on the Jackson case. Danvers had been after him to turn in a brief for the upcoming trial but the MacIntyre business had taken him away from completing it. He decided to put off getting back to Danvers until that afternoon and looked at the third note. It was from Vera Bash. He'd dated her briefly the year before, and although things hadn't worked out— she'd been the one to break off their relationship, something about his job and her needs and a conflict between the two that he didn't understand—they'd promised to stay friends. But keeping that promise had gotten tougher since she'd been seeing some professor, a teaching colleague of hers at Georgetown, for the past couple of months. He'd think about returning her call later, maybe after he talked to Danvers.

The fourth and final message had come in less than twenty minutes ago and was from a woman named Patricia Ineson. Who was that? He stared at the number. Then it dawned on him. The exchange was the same one he'd dialed when he made his initial contact with Durham, Jellersen & Fisk. And William Durham's standoffish secretary had been a Patricia.

He picked up his phone and called.

"William Durham's office," a female voice answered on his third ring.

"Patricia Ineson?" he said.

"Speaking."

"This is Detective John Munch. I—"

"Yes, yes," she said, her voice plunging in volume. "I've been hoping to hear from you this morning."

Munch flitted on an image of her snug sweater and gemlike eyes and wondered if approach three-seventy-seven had been effective after all.

"What can I do for you?" he said, and briefly considered offering a dozen or so suggestions, just to be helpful.

"I can't talk right now," she said quietly. Her words were a little fuzzy, as if she had her lips pressed against the receiver. "Can we meet for lunch? Say twelve-thirty, one o'clock?"

"Okay, let's make it one sharp." His expression had become serious, matching her tone. "You want to get together near your office? I know this place on North Charles—"

"No. Not around here," she said.

"Okay, listen, there's a bar called the Waterfront that I own—well, partially own, a couple of other detectives have shares—anyway, we don't exactly serve haute cuisine, but the burgers are cooked through. It's near the station I work out of—"

"That'd be fine," she said. "May I have the address?"

"Sure," he said. "And free directions to go with it."

Situated on a rebuilt wharf across the street from headquarters, the Waterfront had been in existence for over two hundred years, first as a travelers' inn, later a tavern, then a restaurant, and presently as a tavern-style restaurant. It had a molded tin ceiling, brick walls, overhead fans, a huge mahogany bar, pewter tankards, stool and table seating, and extraordinarily dim lighting, the latter being the most critical feature as far as Munch was concerned. He had wanted the place the minute its previous owner had put it up for sale some three years back, but hadn't had adequate funds for the purchase, what with the alimony payments he was making to his second ex-wife, Maria, not to mention the alimony he'd just finished paying to Gwen, his first ex-wife. The asking price had been so high, in fact, that Munch had had trouble getting up enough cash even after he'd managed to finagle Lewis into going in as his partner, prompting them to seek out yet a third investor, whom they had eventually found in the person of Tim Bayliss.

After some early friction the arrangement had worked out well. The only thing Munch found vaguely dissatisfying about it was that, with three cops running the place, it naturally tended to attract other cops as customers, cops who liked to hang out, swap stories about the job, and generally engage in *cop talk,* which was precisely what he'd hoped working the taps would allow him to get away from once in a while.

"The fact that I tend bar here three times a week gives us something in common right off," he was explaining to Patricia Ineson across a rear table.

"Oh?"

He looked into her gorgeous eyes and tried not to think about ravishing her before their lunch plates arrived.

"This is a historic building, same as the townhouse your illustrious employers call home," he said. "George Washington stopped here once when it was a B&B and there were rooms upstairs."

"Is that so?" she said. "Did he sleep in one of them?"

"Actually, he, um, relieved himself and went on his way," he said. "But I still think it gives us a certain prestige."

The look on her face was equal parts amusement and skepticism.

"The place has a lot of atmosphere," she said. "Very old Baltimore. I can imagine bearded seamen coming in off a big clipper ship, relaxing over their ale after an Atlantic crossing."

"And using the head," he said. "Lest we forget the true source of our reputation, Patricia."

"It's Trish outside the office." She smiled faintly again, then caught her lower lip between her teeth, as if feeling the smile was unsuited to the circumstances that had brought them together. Munch realized her eyes had the same sober look they'd had when she was studying his card the day before.

The waitress brought over their food, a triple-decker turkey club for Munch, soup and salad for Patricia. *Trish.*

"Well, then," he said, biting into his sandwich. "I assume the reason you called me has something to do with Donna MacIntyre's killing."

She nodded and lifted her fork, but didn't touch her food with it.

"The men who run brokerage firms tend to have traditional attitudes and habits," she said, choosing her words. "The nature of the business really demands it."

"I noticed the gentlemanly cuffs on your boss's pants."

She looked at him, no smile this time.

"You should understand that our clients are very refined, very upper-crust—Washington society and longtime political insiders for the most part," she said. "Mr. Durham has his flaws, but it would be unfair to accuse him of pretension because he knows how to package himself, or because you don't happen to like his brand of packaging."

Munch put his sandwich down on his plate.

"Sorry," he said. "Cops always hate their bosses.

Anyone above the rank of lieutenant is pond scum. I forget it isn't the same everywhere."

She nodded and stared quietly down at her salad. It was storming outside again and Munch, facing the door, saw a man and woman come in and take seats at the bar, water sluicing off their raincoats and folded umbrellas. Patricia speared a wedge of tomato with her fork but didn't lift it to her mouth. Munch waited. It struck him that she was deciding how to frame whatever it was she'd come to say.

"Mr. Durham believes in keeping his corporate affairs structured, in avoiding . . . disturbances," she said finally. "He's always viewed getting tangled up in the personal relationships of his subordinates, or other senior executives, as bad policy."

Munch looked at her.

"He claimed yesterday that Donna was likable almost to a fault," he said. "Could it be things weren't quite that rosy?"

"They were in the workplace. People who attain the level of professional status and responsibility that she did often develop massive egos. I've had employers like that and, trust me, they can be unbearable. In Donna MacIntyre's case it would have been especially understandable, given how quickly she rose to her position, and the fact that she was competing in an incredibly male-dominated field. Yet she was one of the most pleasant, upbeat women I've ever met. I think everyone at the office would agree that dealing with her was never a problem."

Munch was still watching her face. "What about outside the office?"

Another beat of silence.

"You're very attentive," she said.

"And I always send flowers on Valentine's Day," he said.

Patricia wasn't smiling. "I don't know if it means anything . . . that is, I did read it was a homeless man who killed Donna . . ."

She let the sentence dangle as though waiting for confirmation from him, but he just sat there neutrally.

After another moment she said, "About three months ago, soon after she was put in charge of our foreign investments division, Donna began meeting with a free-lance consultant in that area named Richard Teel. The financial journals always say he's well respected. Some would add the words charming and handsome to the description."

Munch considered that.

"Donna and Teel became an item," he said.

"That was the rumor, yes," Patricia said. She took a deep breath. "One Monday morning last summer, it wasn't long after I first heard they were involved, Donna showed up for work with bruises on her face. I remember that her eye was swollen, and there was a red welt above her cheek. I also noticed scrapes on her arms. She told everyone she'd been mountain biking and taken a fall, but as a woman I, well, . . ."

She shook her head.

"You didn't believe her?"

"I'm sure the part about having gone biking was

true. She loved athletics, and I'd seen her come back from shopping for gear—gloves, special helmets and shoes, and those little computers bikers put on their handlebars. But I knew she'd gone with Mr. Teel that weekend."

"Did she actually tell you they were together?"

"No. We wouldn't have discussed anything that personal," she said, shaking her head again. "But the Friday before, I'd seen him pick her up when I left the building to go home. He was waiting outside in a jeep-type vehicle, and there were two bicycles on top. In racks, you know." She paused. "Also, Donna was carrying a small suitcase when she came in that day, as if she were heading off on a trip straight from work."

Munch sat there thinking some more. The door opened and let in a gust of chill air and another soggy customer.

He was starting to feel down.

"Are you absolutely convinced Teel hit her?" he said.

"Yes, though I wasn't right away," she said. "Accidents do happen, and Donna never seemed distressed in the way you might expect of a woman who's been assaulted by someone she's dating. But the only time I ever saw Richard Teel again—before this morning, that is—was several weeks later, when he arrived to see her without an appointment. They spoke behind closed doors for a few minutes, and then he left her office, looking so furious he seemed like a different person. This was in late August, or maybe the very beginning of September." She played with her food some more. "There's one last thing you should know. We have in-house security at our firm. Nothing elaborate, just two or three retired police officers under the direction of someone named Walter Silvio. Walter and I talk occasionally, and some weeks ago he told me—in confidence—that Donna wanted him to keep an extra eye out for Mr. Teel, and notify her immediately if he was seen in or around the building."

"You ask him why?"

"No," she said. "The reason seemed obvious."

"Did Durham know all this was happening?"

She looked at him. "He knows everything that goes on in our company."

"And yet he clammed up about it when I spoke to him," Munch said. "Why? Because he figured it was bad for the image?"

"We've already been through that," she said. "I'm sure Mr. Durham would choose to say raising the issue would have been indiscreet."

Munch swallowed another bite of his sandwich. He was used to eating alone and didn't much mind that the lovely, loyal-to-her-boss Patricia Ineson had barely eaten her salad. But her soup, a carrot and ginger bisque that was a house specialty, was also untouched and probably cold by now. This pained him. Gary, the new cook, was the best soup man in town, and it was almost tragic to see his culinary efforts wasted.

"Clear something up for me," he said. "You mentioned a second ago that Teel was at the office this morning, right?"

She nodded slowly, looking down at the table.

"You also said your boss knew Donna had instructed the security people to keep Teel out."

She nodded again.

"That being the case, what was Teel doing there?"

She raised her eyes back to his face and stared at him.

"Donna's gone," she said after a long moment. "And Mr. Durham needs a new vice president."

Less than an hour later Munch was in the Charles Center office of Richard Teel, wondering if he was a goddamn fool for being there. The MacIntyre killing was, after all, Pembleton and Bayliss's crime to investigate. His participation was supposed to have been marginal—a helping hand at the murder scene, notification of the next of kin. The latter having been done as a favor, not that anybody had shown much appreciation. He had his own caseload to worry about, right? The Jackson brief and a dozen other unfinished pieces of business. Moreover, Pembleton and Bayliss had collared their suspect. A bunch of witnesses had made him as the guy who aced MacIntyre. He'd been recognized in a composite sketch and a lineup. A crazed homeless man, not a power executive. Nobody was exactly going to mistake one for the other. Everything had been wrapped up nice and neat. Why didn't he steer clear of it?

As he'd started out through the heavy rain after putting Patricia Ineson in a cab, he had been strongly tempted to do just that: forget the whole affair, walk the short street to headquarters, and bury his head in paperwork. But then he'd remembered the Ernst print hanging in Donna Anne MacIntyre's living room . . . what was it called? *Little Girls Set Out to Hunt the White Butterflies*. That was it. Once the image burst into his mind he'd been unable to get it out: myriad fragments of color coming together, glowing with a light of their own, as if the artist had captured some vital, living force as it trembled at the threshold of *becoming*. Donna Anne MacIntyre had been a success. A strong woman who had made it to the top in an old-time good-old-boy field, by all accounts without trading off any of her warmth and decency. How tough must it have been for her every step of the way? What light was extinguished, what potential snuffed out, when she ceased to be?

Somehow these questions had pushed Munch toward the forty-eighth floor of the towering office complex where he now sat facing Teel, a dark-haired, broad-shouldered, and, yes, handsome and charming man in his middle thirties who looked like a *GQ* cover shot in an imported navy-blue suit with a handkerchief peeking out of the breast pocket, a white shirt, burgundy silk tie, and glistening black wingtips.

"I appreciate your agreeing to meet at such short notice," Munch said. "Hopefully I'll be out of here in a few minutes."

"It's the least I could do after what's happened," Teel said. "Frankly, I'm just a little surprised you wanted to talk to me."

They were on opposite wings of a boomerang-shaped sofa in what Munch guessed was known as the conference area of Teel's inner sanctum—a modern, open office with three glass walls, beige carpeting, and a lot of clean lines and direct lighting. Two steaming cups of coffee sat on the granite table between them. Munch lifted his cup to his mouth and sipped. The coffee was strong, probably an Italian blend.

"Mr. Teel, I'm really just trying to get a little background on Donna MacIntyre. From the people who knew her, you understand."

Teel nodded. "We worked together closely last summer. Donna was getting a new division of Durham off the ground and sought my advice about attracting overseas investors to the U.S. stock market, particularly large-capital Pacific Rim corporations. But I'm sure you already know all that."

"Why?"

"Excuse me?"

"Why are you so sure?"

Teel looked confused.

"Well," he said, "I'm assuming you've spoken with Donna's colleagues at her firm. Who else would've told you about me?"

Munch put his coffee cup down on the table.

"Let's be straight with each other, okay?" he said.

Teel looked at him.

He waited.

Teel looked at him some more and nodded.

"Let's," he said.

"Is it true your relationship with Donna was more than professional?" Munch asked. He leaned forward, his elbows on his lap, hands folded across his knees.

Teel was studying him with narrow intensity.

"It's amazing how people will intrude on the private lives of others," he said. "I don't mean you, Detective, but whoever chose to spread that juicy bit of gossip around."

"That doesn't answer my question."

Teel drank some of his coffee and sighed. "It wasn't anything serious. We'd been spending a great deal of time together and one thing led to another. But it didn't last. There were a few romantic weekends in July and August and, I'm not embarrassed to admit, some mutually entertaining afternoon liaisons. And then it was over."

"The two of you ever go mountain biking together?"

Teel blinked.

"God, this *is* remarkable," he said. "What else do you know about me? If you want a kiss-and-tell of everyone I've dated since high school, I suppose I could write one up for you—"

"Look, I really don't like poking around in your extracurricular affairs," Munch said. "It's just that someone told me Donna came back from that trip pretty banged up."

"Which she did. We were up in the Alleghenies and she took a downhill bend too quickly, went flying over her handlebars. Thankfully she came away with nothing worse than some scrapes and bruises."

"Did a doctor look at her afterward?"

Teel shook his head. "I remember offering to take her to a local hospital, or even the ranger station. Just to be on the safe side. But she assured me some antiseptic and Band-Aids would do the trick, and in fact she was feeling fine soon after we got back to the cabin."

"How do you know that?"

Teel's anger surprised Munch. "Because we gave each other a very healthy fucking that night," he said abruptly. "And did so again the next morning."

They looked at each other for a tense moment. The silence had that odd, sterile quality of neutralized sound that was common to modern offices and always made Munch feel as if he were in a sensory deprivation tank. He watched but did not hear the rain pelting against the floor-to-ceiling windows and wished he were somewhere else.

"I apologize for my crudeness," Teel said, the scowl on his forehead clearing all at once. "But I don't like where this is going. I never laid a hand on Donna. Or any woman." He paused. "Besides, what relevance do these personal matters have to your investigation?"

"If you'd assaulted Donna it wouldn't only have been a personal matter. It would have been a criminal offense."

"You're right, of course. But let's remember that Donna was killed by a homeless derelict."

Munch said nothing to either challenge or endorse that statement.

"Why'd she ask building security at Durham to watch out for you?"

Teel stared at him, shaking his head.

"I thought you were after background information on Donna, yet we're talking as if I'm somehow tied in with her murder," he said. "Who's been giving you an earful, Detective? I'd really like to know."

Munch just shrugged. "About the security notification," he said. "If you don't mind."

Teel sighed again. "I ended the relationship," he said. "As your questions go to show, rumors were circulating, and I was both uncomfortable with that and concerned about how they would impact upon my business dealings. Also, I never really connected with Donna on an emotional level. We got along wonderfully as colleagues, and had an intense physical attraction for each other, but it was clear to me that we had no future together." The downcurved line reappeared between his eyebrows. "Unfortunately, Donna clung, and that's when the problems started."

"What do you mean?"

"We'd agreed to keep work and play separate, and I was under the misconception that we'd be able to continue having a professional relationship after the affair ran its course. My advice and analysis aren't free, and I probably should have insisted that Donna sign a contract for my consulting services, as I'd normally do with any client. But under the circumstances . . ." He shrugged. "Donna's gone, and I don't want to cloud her reputation, but the truth is she took it very hard when I told her it was over. Suddenly I was no longer to be a consultant on her project. Nor was I going to be paid for all the time I'd put into it."

"How much money are we talking about?"

"Well upwards of a hundred thousand dollars," Teel said. "Besides Donna herself, no one had been more involved in structuring her company's new division than I was."

"And you're telling me she had you bounced when you tried to collect?"

"In a nutshell, yes," Teel said. He spread his hands in a gesture that suggested disappointment and regret. "She was afraid of being embarrassed, and became irrationally vindictive. Once she decided to strike out there was no getting through to her."

"You ever talk to Durham or any of the other execs about the money you were owed?"

"Of course not. With nothing in writing, I would have looked foolish. And I felt responsible in part for Donna's erratic conduct. If I'd exposed how she was acting, her superiors would very likely have dismissed her rather than risk a scandal."

Munch contemplated asking Teel about his huddle with Durham that morning, but decided to keep his knowledge of it to himself for the present. He wanted some time to think about this conversation, and about the angry transformation that had stormed across Teel's features when he'd been asked about Donna's supposed biking accident—and his less-than-charming comments at that moment. And then there was the version of Donna Anne MacIntyre he was getting from Teel, a far different one than he'd been presented with until now. Which of them was he to accept, Donna the White, or Donna the Black? Something was off here, though it was an open question whether that made any difference as far as the investigation into her murder was concerned. The person who did it was in custody, wasn't he?

"Mr. Teel, before I go," he said, taking out his pad, "could you give me your whereabouts between six-thirty and seven o'clock Tuesday evening?"

Teel looked incredulous.

"I feel I'd better contact my attorney," he said. "If you're going to treat me as if I'm a suspect—"

"It's really just for the record," Munch lied.

Teel was staring at him in the artificial silence. "A group of Japanese speculators has hired me to help in the expansion of their American holdings and familiarize them with our market practices. Tuesday night I gave them a reception and informational video presentation."

"Where was that?"

"The Whittier Hotel."

"And that can be verified if necessary?"

"By at least a dozen people," Teel said, and suddenly got up off the sofa. "Detective, our chat's lasted longer than I expected, and I have some important calls to make."

He swept his hand toward the far side of the room, indicating a U-shaped electronic console that would have looked at home in Norad Mountain. Behind gray privacy panels, a torrent of financial data was flashing across several large-screen computer displays, while on a lower tier a bank of digital clocks gave readouts of the hour and minute in several key interational time zones. An array of phones and fax machines gave Teel's high-tech command cockpit its finishing touches.

Dismissed, Munch put his notebook back in his pocket and rose, figuring he'd gotten all he was going to get out of Teel anyway. He nodded at the blinking row of clocks.

"Out of curiosity, which of those time zones you phoning?" he asked.

A slight smile appeared at one corner of Teel's mouth.

"All of them," he said.

He spotted her when she was still a block away, hotshit bitch walking toward him with her high heels clicking on the wet sidewalk, strutting under her umbrella like she owned the street, like she had a fucking million-dollar pussy and wanted everybody on the street to know it. Look but don't touch, you can't afford it, ain't *never* gonna afford it, better make a date with your hand, that's what her walk was saying. That's what got him so mad and frustrated, what made him reach inside his pocket and tighten his fingers around the grips. Wearing some kind of expensive coat, short skirt underneath, he'd noticed her legs when the wind had kicked up and the coat flaps had parted a little to reveal her knees and a smooth length of thigh. Smooth white skin in the dark rainy night, was she even wearing stockings? Look but don't touch, don't fucking touch, you want to do that you got to have plenty of money, got to wear an executive suit, got to be a *somebody*. Goddamn right that was the message, she was probably on the way to fuck her rich boyfriend right now.

Uh-huh, gonna see about that, he thought, waiting

in the shadows of an apartment building, hanging back against the corner of the building where the shadows were darkest, drenched from the rain, his long hair and beard dripping, his watchcap clinging to his head like a saturated sponge, his knuckles trembling, trembling, trembling over the grips of the thing in his coat pocket. There was nobody else out on the street and he was breathing hard as she approached, breathing in rapid little snatches and thinking about the other whore, the newspapers making such a big deal over her, the cops asking everybody questions. Who the fuck was she except another strut and jiggle, teasing guys like him with something they had to do without, something guys like him couldn't even get near, something bitches like her would never let guys like him have?

She came walking up to the apartment building, passed within two or three feet of where he stood without noticing him, passed so close he could smell her flowery perfume, passed him right by and then turned into the narrow courtyard leading up to the building's entrance door. So this was home sweet home, what a nice stroke of luck.

She paused just inside the courtyard, reaching into the purse hanging at her side with one hand, holding the umbrella over her head with the other, unaware that he had followed silently along behind her, that he had trapped her right where she lived. There was a small light above the door, but it was set far enough back from the street that nobody on the sidewalk would see what was happening. Nobody would stop him from doing what he was going to do to this hotshit million-dollar pussy, keep him from slitting her open from top to bottom right here in the courtyard of her apartment building.

He rushed up on her, his throat tight, his head hot with fury, pulling the gravity knife out of his coat pocket and releasing the blade with a snap of the wrist, raising the knife, making his *move*—

Suddenly, out of nowhere, there were footsteps behind him in the courtyard, several sets of footsteps running up to him from the street and echoing loudly in the courtyard.

"Police! Drop your weapon!" a male voice yelled, and he turned at once, and saw two plainclothes cops with guns in their hands and their badges hanging from loops around their necks, saw them point the guns at him, and had just enough time to register that *he* was the one who'd been trapped, before a knee slammed into his spine and he was thrown to the pavement, the edge of a hand chopping into the side of his neck.

Stars flared across his vision and his hand went numb and his knife went clattering from his slack, twitching fingers.

"Fuckin' *hurts!*" he grunted.

"Tough," the decoy cop said as she slapped on the cuffs and then patted him down, her knee grinding into his back, her sweet-scented perfume filling his nostrils in the last painful seconds before he lost consciousness.

It was ten o'clock at night.

Pembleton and Bayliss were in the Box with a

bearded, watchcapped homeless guy who had been nabbed by a plainclothes anticrime unit after he'd pulled a knife on a female decoy officer in the courtyard of an apartment building on Light Street.

Shivering miserably, his chair surrounded by a puddle of water that had dripped from his soaking wet clothes, the homeless guy, who called himself Uno, was confessing to the murder of Donna Anne MacIntyre.

"I did it, I killed that fuckin' whore they been writin' about in the papers, and lemme tell you she deserved what she got," he told the detectives. "Showing what she wouldn't never give up, not to somebody like me, not to any guy whose dick wasn't wrapped in a hunnerd-dollar bill."

Pembleton leaned forward with his elbows on the table, his hands tented under his chin.

"Give us the details," he said. "I want you to go over how you did it, step-by-step."

The guy dragged his palm across his lips.

"You got something to drink?" he said.

"After you tell us how you did it."

"How 'bout a smoke?"

"My partner and I both quit a long time ago."

"At least lemme have a fuckin' towel so I can dry myself, man. I'm *freezin'*."

Pembleton just looked at him.

"Okay, okay, forget it." He took a long breath, cleared his throat. "I was on the street there, Howard Street, when I seen her comin', walkin' with that poodle dog—"

"You sure it was a poodle?"

"That's right."

Pembleton snapped Bayliss a meaningful glance.

"Go on," he said.

"Seen her walkin' with that poodle dog like she was somethin' too good for this world, like the fuckin' *dog* was better'n me, an' I couldn't stand it, made me wanna puke." He cleared his throat again. "You sure you can't give me a Coke or somethin'?"

"When you're done," Pembleton said flatly. "Tell me what happened next."

"I cut her," the guy said.

Pembleton and Bayliss exchanged another brief look.

"How?" Pembleton asked.

"What do you mean?"

"How exactly did you cut her?"

"With my fuckin' knife, is how."

"You're saying you stabbed her with a knife?"

"Sure didn't use my little finger," the guy said, and grinned broadly.

"All right, just a minute."

Pembleton stood up, gesturing for Bayliss to follow him into the corridor.

"Give Anticrime a call, tell them they can have their collar back, and that he ought to be booked for attempted assault with a deadly weapon," Pembleton said when they were out of earshot.

"In a way, I suppose we should be glad he's just a copycat," Bayliss said.

"How's that?"

"Goes to show Seth Wilkins is the right man in the MacIntyre killing."

Pembleton shrugged.

"You ask me, it only goes to show this joker isn't," he said.

SEVEN

WHEN LIEUTENANT AL Giardello arrived at the station Friday morning, he found the stairs leading up to the homicide squad room blocked by a phalanx of reporters, photographers, and TV cameramen, and the walls surrounding the stairs bristling with boom mikes covered with furry sound-baffles that resembled, sort of, giant caterpillars.

All this media attention was focused not on the police themselves, but on Wayne Morley and a contingent of his fellow activists from People Now!, a high-profile, often militant group of champions for the homeless that Morley had founded in the mideighties and been figureheading ever since. Standing with them in a show of emphatic solidarity was Deborah Reeves of the public defender's office.

Giardello would later discover that an unknown tipster in the department had notified the press of last night's questioning of a second potential suspect in the

MacIntyre killing, this irresponsible numbskull (in Gee's words) not having subsequently bothered updating his little scoop with information that the knife-wielding homeless man was, in short order, determined to be a copycat by investigators Pembleton and Bayliss. The story, incomplete and misleading as it was, had then been transmitted to the public defender's office by some odious journalistic weasel (also in Gee's words), who had in turn routed it to Wayne Morley. Always one to exploit a spotlight-gaining opportunity, Morley had quickly gathered his troops for an 8 A.M. *putsch*, so to speak, against those cruel oppressors of the poor and downtrodden, the BCPD.

"We all are horrified by the murder of an innocent woman, and we all want to find the person who is guilty of having committed the crime! But in seeking justice for Donna Anne MacIntyre, must we do *in*justice to others?" Morley was declaring to the reporters as Gee pushed into the congested stairwell. A short, stocky man with a fringe of reddish-brown hair around a gleaming pink pate, wearing a sacklike khaki shirt and baggy brown pants, Morley resembled nothing so much as a tonsured monk standing there in front of the microphones.

"Every human life is precious!" Morley intoned piously. "Is fairness something we reserve for men and women with well-paying jobs, and roofs over their heads, and soft beds to sleep on, or will it be equally applied to those who long for a modest day's wage, and whose only roof is the sky, and only bed is a hard square of concrete? If not, my friends, then we may as well strike the word *fair* from the dictionary, because it's truly lost all meaning!"

Giardello thought this was laying it on ridiculously thick, although several of the newshounds applauded, and one op-ed columnist he knew actually gave Morley a clenched-fist salute.

He clung to the handrail and sidled up the stairs, hoping he'd make it to his office unnoticed, and wondering where Pembleton and Bayliss, who'd been pulling double-duty the past few days, were hiding out.

"Is it your belief that Seth Wilkins is being wrongly accused?" a reporter asked Morley.

"What I believe is that the police must abide by the laws of our society, and that the law must never be enforced arbitrarily. What I believe is that people shouldn't be targeted as suspects, even entrapped, simply because they are without means. And what I *know* is that not one, but *two* homeless men have been arrested and interrogated in connection with this murder without sufficient evidence linking either to the crime. A line must be drawn here and now on behalf of the powerless and destitute!"

Morley raised his hands in the air, palms upward, and gesticulated emotionally . . . which, Giardello had to admit, made him look even more like a mendicant friar than before.

"I ask you, does pinning a badge over a man's heart shield it from decency and compassion?" he said, pulling out all his rhetorical stops now. "How are we to react when authorities who've been trusted with the public welfare blatantly *violate* that trust and—?"

"Just a minute!" Giardello blurted, and suddenly found himself facing a thicket of microphones and cameras.

He frowned, realizing he'd been expertly jerked. Why on *earth* weren't Pembleton and Bayliss out here with him?

"Lieutenant Giardello!" a reporter from the *Sun* shouted, recognizing him. "Would you like to comment on Mr. Morley's statement?"

"All I want to say is that, in spite of the asinine remarks I've just heard, the police department is here to protect *every* resident of this city, and that our standards of fairness do not change for any person or reason."

"Has Wilkins been formally indicted?"

"No, but—"

"What about the second homeless man apprehended last night?"

"He was brought in on serious assault charges unrelated to the MacIntyre case, but the very fact that we questioned him about it should prove we're keeping open minds, and exploring every possible lead."

"*Was* he a victim of police entrapment?"

Giardello rolled his eyes, incensed. "It was *he* who attacked a plainclothes officer with an eight-inch knife, and *not* the other way around! We all ought to be thankful he went after a trained policewoman with backup rather than someone's helpless wife or daughter."

"Lieutenant, can you tell us what specific evidence you've gathered against Seth Wilkins?"

"I won't discuss that during an ongoing investigation."

"According to Mr. Morley—"

"I don't give a *damn* what else that self-celebrating idiot has said, and furthermore I question his right to hold an unannounced press conference in a government building!"

Morley gave him a pitying look across the stairs, as though Giardello were the most wretched sinner in existence.

"Lieutenant, please, don't be unreasonable," he called out magnanimously, thrusting his face toward a camera lens. "Rather than continue widening the schism between the haves and have-nots, it might be best for us to examine this problem in an open forum. A televised debate, for instance—"

"I've got a job to do, Morley, and I'm sure you'd rather hear *yourself* talk anyway!" Giardello roared in a startling baritone.

And without awaiting a response, he pushed past a cluster of microphones and jostled his way up the remaining stairs to the squad room in seething silence.

Their backs to the staircase, Pembleton and Munch were standing beside Bayliss's desk as Giardello entered the room.

"I swear to *God,* the three of you better not be monkeying around with card tricks," he bellowed, storming up behind them. "Do any of you know what I just had to handle alone?"

The detectives turned to face him.

"Actually we all got here before Morley did," Bayliss said, peering up at Gee from his chair.

"And have been comparing notes on the MacIntyre case," Munch said.

"Which we believe serves a better purpose than adding to the hubbub downstairs," Pembleton said.

Giardello looked at them, still fuming.

"Somebody could have warned me I'd be running into an ambush!" he hollered, directing this particular war cry at the coffee room, where Howard, Lewis, and Kellerman were doing their best not to be seen.

"That would've meant one of us goin' down there, an' probably havin' to answer some reporter's stupid questions," Lewis said through a bite of his Pop Tart. "Figured we should leave that to you, bein' you're our leader."

"And a very diplomatic leader, besides," Kay said.

"Who's also quick on his feet," Kellerman said.

Giardello glared at them.

"Try showering me with adulation when I'm not so pissed off," he said, and turned back to Pembleton and company. "I want the MacIntyre case handed over to the D.A. by noon. Maybe an indictment will put an end to all this damn speculation about . . ."

Giardello lost the rest of the sentence, having suddenly noticed the hesitant expressions that had fallen over the three detectives' faces.

"What is it?" he asked.

"Well, . . ." Munch said.

"Uh, . . ." Bayliss said.

"Munch has some ideas," Pembleton said.

"What kind of ideas?"

"It gets complicated," Pembleton said.

"Really?" Giardello said edgily, shooting Munch a look.

"It's just that I've got a gut feeling . . ."

"Oh, I think I'm going to *love* this."

". . . that maybe we ought to look at Donna MacIntyre's killing from a different angle. Before we prosecute somebody who might be innocent."

Giardello shook his head.

"I refuse to believe I'm hearing this," he said. "We have a solid case against Wilkins. . . . For God's sake, there are multiple eyewitnesses. . . ."

"None of whom actually saw him pull the trigger," Bayliss said.

"Also, there's something about the gun that was used," Pembleton said.

"What *about* it?"

"I got a rush report from Ballistics that confirms it's either a Walther or a similar European firearm. Not the kind of heat you'd expect a guy without a nickel to his name would be packing."

"He could've stolen it."

"Could have," Pembleton said, "although he has no record of previous first or second felonies."

"No jacket at all, for that matter," Bayliss said.

"Look, every one of your witnesses saw him take off running immediately after they heard the gunshots. A couple saw a weapon in his hand. And there wasn't anybody else near the victim."

"Or maybe there was and none of them spotted him," Bayliss said. "It was a dark night."

"It's even possible Wilkins bolted because he saw the real killer and panicked," Pembleton said.

Giardello looked at Munch again. "How do you explain the gun?"

"I don't know," Munch said. "Listen, maybe he's guilty. *Probably,* okay? But there's this guy Donna was going out with that seriously rubs me the wrong way, and it's pretty clear he got violent with her before they broke up . . . and might've been stalking her afterward. Yet Donna's boss, who's tied in professionally with the guy, is covering up for him. Or not volunteering information about him, anyway."

"Why would he be keeping secrets?"

"That's where the path starts to get winding," Munch said. "I already spoke to him once, and thought I'd pay him another visit later today. Maybe I can get him to tell me what he knows."

"Who's the boyfriend?"

"Some highfalutin stock market analyst name of Richard Teel," Munch said. "He has a Charles Center office that looks like it was decorated by George Lucas."

"Are you saying you think *he* killed her?"

"He's got an alibi that I still need to check out," Munch said. "But, like I said, there's something off about him, and I want to know what it is before putting some whacked-out hard luck case on trial for murder."

"Rich man, poor man," Giardello muttered, rubbing the back of his neck.

The detectives waited.

"All right," he said finally. "We can hold off on an indictment for another twenty-four hours. After that, either we get one or Wilkins strolls. And if he does, you all know as well as I do that he's liable to disappear into a black hole. This is a homeless drifter we're talking about . . . as our crusading friend Morley's busy telling all those cameras downstairs."

He took a long, slow breath, looking steadily at the three of them.

"Twenty-four hours," he repeated. "And I damn well hope you bring me something more than gut feelings."

At his own desk shortly after receiving Giardello's deadline pronouncement, Munch got the phone number of the Whittier Hotel out of the directory and called to see if anybody there could corroborate Teel's story about the business reception.

The desk clerk didn't know anything. She transferred him to the hotel manager, who also didn't know anything. The hotel manager put him onto the food and beverage director, who *did* have knowledge of the reception, which, he recalled, had been booked in Teel's name—actually, in the name of his firm, Teel Financial Analysis—for five-thirty the previous Tuesday evening. Although he hadn't been present for the affair, he was able to give Munch a list of service personnel who did work the room, including a table captain, two waiters, a bartender, and a bus boy.

". . . According to my schedule, the captain and

bartender are on for lunch today, if you want to come down and talk to them," he said. "Ought to be here any minute to start setting up."

Munch told him he'd be right over, hung up the phone, got his coat, grabbed Bayliss's coat and umbrella off the rack, tossed them to him, and left the squad room with Bayliss in tow, explaining where they were going, and why they were going there, as they hustled down a back stairwell to avoid the Morley-Reeves dog-and-pony show still in progress out front.

After a fifteen-minute walk through the teeming rain—which had persisted into a fourth day with no break in sight—they got to the hotel, met the food and beverage man in his office, and then were led into a small fifth-floor conference room and introduced to the two staffers who had waited on Teel and his guests.

"Sure I remember the reception," the captain, whose name was Henry Robbins, said in response to Munch's initial question. "Party of fifteen. They were executives from Japan."

"Except for Mr. Teel, naturally," added the bartender, whose name was Joseph Madrazo.

Robbins was tall and thin with short blond hair. Madrazo was tall and thin with short black hair. Both had on their work threads and were smoking Kools. If not for their hair color being different it would have been hard to tell them apart.

"And everything got started on time?" Munch asked.

Robbins nodded. "Cocktails and canapés at five-thirty, Teel's presentation at six-thirty, tea and coffee at seven."

"Cocktails and what?" Bayliss asked.

"Canapés, Timmy," Munch said, hoping against hope that he was not about to be embarrassed.

"Oh," Bayliss said. "You mean, like, ladyfingers, right? And those cocktail franks with that sort of doughy crust around them?"

Munch winced. Score another one for the image of the cop as low-rent boob, he thought disgustedly.

"More like salmon mousse, shad roe, and beluga caviar," Robbins said, suppressing either a grin or a frown, it was a tough call. "The Whittier is a first-class hotel, Detective."

"Oh, I see," Bayliss said.

"What was the arrangement like?" Munch asked.

"We used a large conference room for the reception," Robbins said. "Afterward they went into an adjoining room for Mr. Teel's presentation. He'd asked us to hook up a VCR and big-screen television ahead of time, which is, you know, pretty standard these days."

"Were you around for the entire shebang?"

"Well, I oversaw everything while the food was being served, and Joey here would've been at the bar. . . ."

"What about Mr. Teel? Did either of you see him leave the reception at any time?"

They both shook their heads.

"I would have noticed if he stepped out," Robbins said. "It might sound a little odd, but part of my job is to keep an eye on the host of an affair. To make sure he looks happy with the food and service, and how everything is going in general. This was a smallish group, so it was easy."

"And you're also saying he stuck around?" Munch asked the bartender. "Just to make sure I'm getting it straight."

"He was there the whole time."

"Drinking much?"

Madrazo wobbled his hand in a gesture that meant so-so.

"He had vodka and tonics, came back for maybe three refills," Madrazo said. "Wanted Stoli or nothing."

"After the reception, when the Japanese guys went into the other room to watch the video, did Teel go with them?" Bayliss asked.

Robbins nodded.

"Everything right on schedule?"

"As I told you, that's how we do things," Robbins said, looking mildly affronted by the question.

"Were any food or drinks served during the presentation?" Munch asked.

"No, and that's also very typical," Robbins said. "Once the guests are conducting business, you leave them alone . . . unless of course there's a special request, which in this instance there wasn't."

"And the presentation ran how long, again?"

"From six-thirty to seven. Although they were all seated for it by six-fifteen."

"Where were you guys during that hour or so?"

"Well, Joey was cleaning up the bar, and I would have been supervising preparations for tea and dessert."

"This is back in the first room?" Bayliss asked.

"That's right."

"Could Teel, or anyone else in the group, have left for any period while the showing was in progress?" Munch asked.

"If you mean when the video was running, I doubt it," Robbins said. "It seems to me that would be very unusual, anyway."

"But is it possible?" Munch persisted.

"Well, sure. Occasionally people have to use the rest rooms, you know. Or someone's beeper goes off and he leaves to make a phone call. But, really, unless it was some emergency I don't think Mr. Teel would've gone out during his own presentation."

"Why's that?" Bayliss said. "I mean, once the tape's in the machine, what's he have to do?"

"It isn't that, Detective," Robbins said, and expelled a sigh. "I'm talking about your basic good form. Businessmen from Asian countries are especially concerned with manners, and Mr. Teel is topflight."

Munch considered the last part of his answer.

"Teel's had this sort of gathering at the hotel before?"

"Absolutely," the table captain said. "Very often, in fact."

Munch nodded and scribbled a note into his pad.

"You said dessert was at seven, right?" he asked.

"Yes."

"And it started on time, of course."

"Of course."

"Anyone leave early?"

"No."

"When was the last time you saw Teel?"

"I'd say it must have been around a quarter to eight. He went out to the elevators with his guests."

"Okay," Munch said, and thought a moment. "Getting back to the video presentation . . . if anyone *had* by any chance left while the tape was running, who would know?"

Robbins shrugged. "Well, nobody's going to make an announcement if they need to use the men's room—"

"I'm talking about leaving the hotel, not going to take a leak," Munch interrupted, a little tired of the guy's puffed-up attitude.

Robbins seemed puzzled by his annoyance.

"My guess is the doorman would be aware of something like that. Possibly the coat check girl, too." He sighed again. "I can't think of anyone else, offhand."

"They around now?"

Robbins shook his head. "Their shift wouldn't start till three o'clock this afternoon. The members of my waiting staff alternate between lunches and dinners, but all the other employees are on set schedules."

Munch jotted something else in his pad and closed it.

"Anything else either of you want to mention?" he

said. "Did anybody at the reception act funny, or say something that sticks out in your minds?"

Madrazo was shaking his head, but Robbins just sat there looking kind of blank.

"What is it?" Munch asked him.

"Nothing important," he said, shrugging again.

"How about you let us decide that?" Bayliss said.

"Well, Mr. Teel was a little, I don't know, *touchy,* let's say, with the staff after the presentation. We served eight or ten different types of tea—his clients were Japanese, you understand—but even though it was our usual brand, he complained about the type of green tea we used."

"What did you make of it?"

"Nothing at all, to tell you the truth . . . and I still don't, which is why I wasn't going to bring it up," Robbins said. "I just wondered if the presentation had gone well. Mr. Teel's profession can be very demanding, you know . . . and he's the kind of person who wants to be number one in everything."

It was about a ten-minute drive from the Whittier Hotel to the Mt. Vernon offices of Durham, Jellersen & Fisk when traffic was moving, although you could also ride the bus or trolley, both of which took longer but eliminated the need to find parking. So did cabbing it, of course, if you could catch a taxi that wasn't already occupied. And then there was also the subway.

As it happened, Munch and Bayliss wound up walking through the torrential downpour rather than taking any of these means of transportation. Fully a third of the unmarked cars used by the homicide unit were in the shop for repairs, most with electrical problems resulting from the Niagra of water that had been spilling from the heavens over the past few days. The remaining cars had been grabbed by other detectives before Munch got to the yard that morning, leading him to suspect the requisitions officer was playing favorites with people, and that neither he nor Bayliss was presently on his good side. The busses and trolleys had presented another sort of problem in that they'd been running hours late due to street flooding of near-biblical proportions. And trying to flag down an available cab during a rainstorm in *any* city was a fool's endeavor. With car, cab, and bus ruled out, Munch had seen no option left but the train.

Bayliss, however, deep-sixed that one.

"You won't catch me going into the hole," he explained as they had splashed across town under their umbrellas. "No way."

"Pembleton's right about you," Munch said. "You are an antisubway snob."

"It's got nothing to do with snobbery," Bayliss said. "First of all, I hate being packed in with crowds."

"Rush hour's over, Timmy."

"I wasn't finished with my reasons," Bayliss said. "Step aboard a train, and you're trusting your life to a conductor you never even see, who's got his hands on controls you wouldn't recognize if your life depended on it. What if he drops dead while you're chugging down the tracks at forty miles an hour?"

"There's a heart-attack switch, or lever, or something like that in the cabin. He lets go of it for any reason, the train stops."

"You sure about that?"

"Positive."

"Well, I'll admit that's reassuring, but my other doomsday scenario's even scarier," Bayliss said. "Picture this, okay? Some nut with an AK or an Uzi under his coat—let's say a postal clerk who's had a mental breakdown—steps aboard your car, waits till you're between stations, and opens up, *ratta-tat-tat*. That happens, you're stuck. Nowhere to go." Bayliss shivered. "And don't start with your wisecracks about how I could make the guy's weapon disappear with a magic wand, because even talking about this gives me the creeps. Something like it actually happened in New York, remember?"

Munch had briefly paused to look at him in the pouring rain.

"Congratulations," he said.

"For what?"

"For having joined me in the deep, dark geek-pit of incapacitating neurosis," he said.

Bayliss thought about what to say to that, and found himself unable to come up with anything.

Still, he was quietly troubled by Munch's comments for the remainder of their walk, and was about to finally ask whether or not he'd been serious, when Munch came to an abrupt halt in front of the building to which they'd been journeying through the rain, a look of sharp interest on his face as he saw who was walking out the door.

He'd intended to have a second talk with Durham this morning. What he hadn't expected was to nearly collide with Richard Teel on his way into Durham's townhouse.

"Well, who'd have guessed," he said, his eyes lifted to where Teel had paused on the steps, raindrops bouncing and spattering off his huge umbrella.

Wearing a natty London Fog trench coat and matching fedora, carrying an attaché case that Munch figured cost almost what he himself earned in a month, Teel stood there doing his best not to seem flustered.

"Hello, Detective Munch," he said. "Strange to see you here."

"Guess you got back the keys to the kingdom," Munch said.

Teel smiled, too quickly.

"It's no coincidence that my visit comes so soon after our conversation yesterday," he said. "After you left my office, I couldn't stop thinking about what happened to Donna, and realized it was important to personally set matters straight with Mr. Durham. And, of course, extend my condolences." He was staring at Munch as he spoke. "It's only a shame the differences that came between Donna and me weren't resolved long ago."

"Sure," Munch said. "Why burn bridges when you don't have to?"

The edges of Teel's smile tightened a little.

"So, Detective, what's your purpose for coming here in this god-awful weather?"

"Believe it or not, I find the rain kind of invigorating," Munch said, and put his hand on Bayliss's shoulder. "Besides, we've decided to start up a portfolio."

Teel just kept smiling. His eyes stuck to Munch's.

"Would you like some expert advice?" he said. "In this instance it's free of charge."

Munch looked back at him through a rippling curtain of rain.

"Sure," he said. "Be dumb not to listen to a smart guy like you."

"Use your common sense and don't speculate," Teel said. "From what I know about policemen's wages, that would only leave you open to serious problems." His smile had suddenly vanished. "Maybe what you should be doing instead is building your case against the piece of trash that killed Donna. Unless, of course, Wayne Morley's tactless performance at police headquarters has made it politically incorrect to hold him accountable for his crime."

"Well," Munch said, and shook his head, "I guess that means you feel we should've stayed away from here today."

Teel shrugged and then walked the rest of the way down the steps.

"People can do anything they want with my suggestions," he said. "It's just a shame to see them waste their time and energy."

They stood looking at each other a second or two, rain hissing in the air around them. Then Teel smiled his stiff little smile again, tipped his head sideways at Bayliss, and briskly walked off.

The detectives watched him hail a cab and slide into it.

"How's *he* get one of them to stop?"

"The guy rates, Tim. That's all there is to it," Munch said, and started up the steps.

Although the St. Ignatius soup kitchen would not open its doors until 6 P.M., the cooks were already down in the parish hall at noon, commencing with preparations for the long lines of desperately hungry people who showed up for the free meal program every Tuesday and Friday.

"It's unbelievable how much work there is to do," one of them was telling Pembleton.

A portly, almost hairless man in his sixties named Danny Jusko, wearing a white apron over a crew-necked tee shirt, he had just explained that he'd been head chef at a seafood restaurant in Little Italy before his retirement, but had never had to work as hard for his pay as he did now that he was volunteering his time at the program.

"I mean, two hundred starving mouths, you have the slightest idea what it takes to feed them?" he went on, peeling a potato as he spoke.

"I can see that it's a lot," Pembleton said, and nodded his chin at the huge pyramid of potatoes to Jusko's left, its stability a skillful balancing act that might have drawn approving looks from the architects of ancient Giza. No less impressive was the kitchen itself, which was as well equipped as that of any good restaurant, with a walk-in refrigerator, commercial ovens and ranges, a big steel sink, long cutting counters, and skillets and kettles hanging from grid hooks overhead.

"That's a couple hundred pounds of spuds right there, and not even grade-A goods. Makes cutting and peeling them a real pain since they're not a uniform size and shape."

"I'd imagine."

"But what you gonna do? On our budget you gotta look at bulk, not quality. That means buying vegetables that're farm seconds. We talked a local supermarket into donating the meat we use in our stews—last-day-of-sale stuff, but not bad, all things considered."

"Uh-huh."

"Peeling potatoes, though, that's a job that takes forever, which is why most guys hate it, and why it was one of those punishments you got when you ticked off your sarge in the army," Jusko said. "Me, I can't say I mind it."

"This is all very interesting, sir," Pembleton said, anxious to get to the purpose of his visit. "But—"

"Now, Johnny Burke over there"—Jusko pointed his knife at a thin old man across the room who was chopping onions from a mound that nearly rivaled the potato pyramid in size—"Johnny'd do anything to avoid peeling potatoes, but he doesn't mind onions. You'll never see him tearing up while he's doing it, and from what he says his eyes don't even sting, not even when he's dicing real fine. My entire forty years as a professional, I never could stand working with onions."

"Mr. Jusko—"

"I guess the potato peeling relaxes me, is what it is. Gives me a chance to think about things. Sometimes I bring in a cassette player and listen to tapes, mostly swing and classical music. My daughter bought it for me for Christmas—the tape player, I mean—"

"Mr. Jusko, forgive me for rushing you along, but I *am* investigating a homicide . . ."

"Right, I know, you mentioned that—"

". . . and would really like to ask you a few questions."

Jusko nodded, scooped a heap of loosely coiled peelings off the counter with his hands, dumped them into a trash bag, and reached for another potato.

"Sure," he said, lifting his knife and digging an eye out of the potato. "This about that guy Seth Wilkins, by the way?"

"Matter of fact, it is."

"Figured. Read about the case in the paper. And then this morning on the news—that's *radio* news, you understand, I won't put on the TV during the day—this morning I heard that guy Morley talking at the police station." He shook his head without looking up from his work, a ribbon of potato skin winding from his hands in a perfect spiral. "It's a tragedy all ways 'round. For the girl that got killed *and* the poor guy that did it. I mean, with mental problems like his, he should never have been out on the street in the first place."

"Mr. Jusko—"

"You know, he was here the night it happened,"

Jusko said, taking the question right out of Pembleton's mouth.

Pembleton looked at him.

"You certain about that?"

"Absolutely," Jusko said. "He comes almost every night we're open."

"And there isn't any chance you're confusing him with someone else who fits his general description?"

"His name's Seth, right?"

"Yes."

"Well, then, it's gotta be him."

"Sir," Pembleton said, "you understand how important it is that there be no mistake here . . ."

"Well, I *gather* this is important—"

"Because Wilkins has had many different aliases—"

"The name he gave me every Tuesday night was Seth. Fridays he was Jake. Depending when he catches you, he was a soldier in Vietnam, Iraq, probably even Korea and World War Two," Jusko said. "That sound like him?"

Pembleton nodded. Live and learn. He'd had no idea the guard at the homeless shelter had meant it literally when he'd said Wilkins used a different name for every night of the week.

"Do you remember what time Wilkins arrived?"

"I don't know," Jusko said. "You have to realize, things get busy. Like I already might've told you, we're feeding hundreds of people. There's no time to watch the clock."

"How about a guesstimate?"

Jusko's brow creased thoughtfully as he finished

peeling the potato in his hands and took another from the pyramid.

"Best I can do is say between six and seven."

"How about what time he left?"

"That I really couldn't tell you."

"You can't be *any* more precise?"

"Uh-uh."

"You think any of the other cooks could?"

"I doubt they'll be able to help you any better than I can," Jusko said, shaking his head.

Pembleton was disappointed. He had clocked the walk from the church to the crime scene by taking it himself, and had reached it in less than fifteen minutes, using neither the quickest nor the slowest route, and moving along at a moderate but steady clip. Since the killing had occurred at approximately six-thirty, Jusko's approximation only meant Wilkins had had long enough to commit the murder and get his meal, or get his meal and commit the murder, and, either way, sign in at the shelter by eight, which was the time noted in the admissions register there.

In other words, Jusko's confirmation that Wilkins ate at the soup kitchen the night of the killing proved nothing.

"I think I better talk to the others anyway," he said.

Jusko shrugged, still peeling.

"Good luck," he said. "I'd stay away from Johnny Burke if I were you, though. Those onions of his are potent."

Patricia Ineson sat in the reception room wearing pale

blue eye shadow, a sunflower-yellow blouse with the top three buttons open, and a silky purple scarf around her neck. Munch smelled the soft scent of her perfume as he entered from the hall, and considered telling her she was a rare and magnificent orchid who only grew fairer in the rain. On the other hand, and contrary to popular belief, humiliation wasn't something he actually sought out from members of the opposite sex.

"Good morning, Trish," he said instead.

"Hello, Detective," she said, looking at him from behind her desk. "And it's Patricia while I'm at work."

"Sorry, I forgot," he said, and introduced Bayliss.

Bayliss gave her a rapturous smile.

"Guess who we ran into outside the building?" Munch said.

She faced him at once. "I thought you might cross paths with Mr. Teel. He called and made an appointment late yesterday afternoon."

"Probably right after my visit with him," Munch said.

"Quite a coincidence," she said, "but he's a man who always knows which matters should take precedence over others."

"It's also quite a coincidence that you happened to schedule our meetings back to back, don't you think?"

She gave him a significant look. He wanted to tell her she was a flower in heaven's high bower.

"Mr. Durham's ready to see you," she said after a moment, and showed them to the inner office.

Durham rose from behind his desk when they

entered, motioning them into a pair of plump leather armchairs.

"Please have seats, gentlemen," he said, smiling. "I'm glad to see you again, Detective Munch."

"Sure you are," he said, not returning the smile.

Durham's heavy pink cheeks dropped in a bewildered frown. Munch recognized the look from their first meeting, and supposed it was his standard defense when he wanted to avoid owning up to things he'd done and regretted. Or felt he ought to regret.

"You'll have to pardon me for asking, but is there some problem?" Durham said.

"I think you can answer that for yourself," Munch said, and looked at him awhile without saying anything else.

Durham reached for the letter opener in front of him and began his nervous tapping. As he did, the arm of his suit jacket rode slightly up his shirtsleeve and gave Munch a glimpse of gold cuff links.

"You have heard about Richard Teel," he said at last. His eyes had filled.

Munch nodded. "Why didn't you tell me about him and Donna?"

Durham tapped out several more beats of silence.

"It would be good to know what to do in every situation," he said. "Sometimes it can be difficult, however."

"Teel beat the hell out of her less than two months ago," Munch said. "She was so afraid of him that she asked your security people not to let him in the building. And you had to *wonder* if that information

166

might be important to a cop investigating her murder?"

"Things always have to be weighed," Durham said. "My understanding was, and is, that her killer had been apprehended. I just didn't see the point in bringing up issues that seemed irrelevant."

"I've heard that before," Bayliss said. "Take it down the hall, huh?"

Durham looked at him. "The reference doesn't escape me. But this isn't about some crass Los Angeles star who was indulged by everyone around him, and I can't agree with the comparison."

"Show me the distinction," Munch said. "And while we're at it, let's hear why you've been throwing an open house for Teel practically from the minute Donna wound up on a morgue slab."

Durham was shaking his head.

"It isn't at all like that," he said. "I wish you understood how much Donna meant to me and my partners in New York. She was a quality person, and cannot be given enough credit for moving us into competition with giant underwriters such as Solomon and Goldman, Sachs. No one was more knowledgeable about the intricacies of the market." He paused, sighed. "Richard Teel comes close."

"And nature abhors a vacuum," Munch said. "So you offer Teel Donna's old job, and don't let a pesky little detail like the fact that he assaulted her, or worse, bother you. That's what I call appreciation."

"Again, Detective, I feel you're misreading me. Perhaps I'm something of a traditionalist, but I've never felt comfortable getting involved in the personal lives of the men and women in my employ—"

"For God's sake," Bayliss broke in suddenly. "It isn't like you only closed your eyes to seeing Teel leave Donna's office with lipstick on his collar, or the two of them taking long lunches together. I'd figure you'd want to know why she came to work all cut and bruised after spending a weekend with him."

Durham's face flushed. He opened his mouth to say something, but then just closed it and leaned forward and sat there watching his hand tap his desk with the paper knife.

"I think you did know, sir," Munch said. "There's no way you couldn't have. Not after Donna went to your security man with her problem."

"You've spoken to Silvio, then," Durham said flatly.

"Not yet, but we want to do that while we're here," Bayliss said.

Durham nodded, seemingly less to Bayliss than to himself. His head was still bowed and the tapping had gotten harder and faster. So had his breathing.

"A little over a month ago," he said, "Donna asked Silvio to deny Mr. Teel access to this building, and to have him immediately escorted out in the event he somehow got through the door. She was very agitated at the time, and told him Teel had been intimidating her over the phone, both at home and at work. That he had become . . . aggressive . . . in her office."

He fell silent a moment, tapping, his cheeks puffing in and out with each rapid breath.

"Silvio reported this to me for approval, and I

indicated that he do as Donna requested," he resumed. "Stories get around, and it was an open secret that she'd been having a relationship with Teel. Such things inevitably lead to complications. Teel was a valuable asset when she began organizing the foreign trade division, and I won't say I wasn't concerned that their falling out might short-circuit the development process. But Donna was the single most important officer in this firm other than the partners themselves, and I wasn't going to override her instructions."

"Did Teel stay away from her after that?" Bayliss asked.

"I thought so," Durham said. "But then . . ."

His head bowed a little lower. His cheeks were now a deep red. He almost looked like he was hyperventilating.

"Yes?" Munch prompted.

"The morning before Donna was killed, she approached me in confidence and said Teel had gone on trying to make contact with her. There had been more phone calls. And he'd begun writing her threatening letters. She brought a manila envelope full of them into my office with her."

"You still have them?"

He shook his head.

"I passed the envelope along to Silvio without opening it. I've been negotiating the terms of an offering for the past couple of weeks, and thought Silvio could read the letters and review their content for me at a less hectic time. I'm sure he held onto them."

"What else did Donna tell you?"

"On several recent occasions Teel showed up where she lived. She said he wouldn't try going into her building because there was a doorman, and because her sister was staying with her, but that he would wait for her on the street nearby, or sometimes in the subway kiosk she would exit returning home from work. She said he would insist she give him another chance, and become enraged when she rejected him."

"Why'd she come to you that day? Was she thinking you could help her straighten things out?"

"Yes," Durham said. "Donna felt that unless his harassment stopped she would have to go to the police, but she knew I'd want to avoid a needless scandal and hoped I could handle the matter quietly. Perhaps have Silvio warn him off. She apparently felt that Teel had emotional problems relating to his military service, and that they were intensifying—"

"Hold it." Munch put up his hand. "Before you go any further, *what* military service?"

"From what I know, he was with the Special Forces Rangers, and saw action in Panama and Desert Storm. Beyond that, I'm afraid I really can't be specific."

The detectives glanced at each other. Both could feel their hearts racing.

"I don't get it," Bayliss said. "You're a bright guy. With everything you know about Teel, everything Donna told you, how is it you haven't asked yourself if he could've been involved in her death?"

Durham looked up at him, the hand that held the paper knife suddenly motionless, his face trembling.

"You make it sound as though I've been covering up for a murderer," he said. "That isn't true."

The detectives waited for an answer to the question.

"You may not understand my offering Teel Donna's position, may not agree with it, but I've always made a solid distinction between the way men and women conduct themselves in the workplace, and what happens when they form romantic entanglements."

The detectives kept waiting for an answer.

"I see your point," Durham said finally. "Of course I wondered about Teel. At first. But when I heard about the homeless man . . . when I heard there had been an arrest, I was relieved. I became convinced my suspicions were unfounded. Convinced he wasn't involved."

Munch and Bayliss looked at each other again, neither of them commenting. Then, after what seemed like a long while, Munch turned back to Durham.

"Maybe," he said, "that's exactly what Teel wanted."

EIGHT

(1)

10/25

D.A.,

 Not being able to see you at the office is really getting me down.

 By now you must realize that what I did, I did <u>for your own good.</u> You said yourself that you're not as focused in your personal life as you'd like. Maybe that's why we hit it off from the very beginning. My years as an Army Ranger taught me to seize control 110% of the time, and I tried to impart some of that discipline to you. I thought that was what you wanted and needed. I thought that, together, we could <u>both have everything we ever wanted.</u> Without you, I feel I'm only half as good as I ought to be.

 I love you, babe. Through thick and thin. No relationship, no matter how solid, is without its hard times. We're both passionate people so we can both be explosive. Like that weekend in the Alleghenies, and then last week, when you wouldn't talk to me outside your building—you pushed my buttons, and I got a little rough. I admit that, okay?

> *The thing is, though, you've been trying to hide from your own emotions, and I have to make you see that. You're a strong, and occasionally <u>strong-willed,</u> woman, but don't set yourself moving in a direction that <u>CANNOT BE.</u> There is no one else for you. There will never be anyone else for me. Without each other there is truly <u>no reason for EITHER OF US to exist</u> . . . and we both know I can find a way to end it all if necessary. Oblivion would be better than life in an uncaring world.*
>
> *As I said on the message I left on your answering machine last night (where WERE you at 10 p.m.? I'm trying not to believe the worst, trying not to believe you've been with another man . . . but you should have been home) the ball is in your court now. YOU control both our destinies. . . .*

LOVE YOU <u>FOREVER,</u>
Richard.

"The guy's a fake. It's like he made up this character for himself, and just goes around acting the part, you know," Walter Silvio was saying. "Richard Teel, Super Soldier. Or maybe Secret Agent. I haven't decided which."

It was 1:37 P.M.

Five minutes earlier, Munch and Bayliss had left William Durham's third-floor executive stronghold and gone downstairs to the far less elegant basement office from which Silvio directed building security, such as it was.

Now Munch placed the letter dated October 25—written only a week ago, three days before Donna Anne MacIntyre was killed—on top of the stack he had gotten out of a brown nine-by-eleven-inch envelope, the same envelope Donna had given her boss when she'd appealed for protection from a man who was clearly exhibiting dangerous tendencies—and whose problems had been rapidly coming to a boil following his breakup with Donna, judging by the ultimatum expressed in his writing.

"What makes you say that?" Munch asked. "About him being a fraud, that is."

Silvio gave him a small, knowing smile. A former training sergeant with the BCPD, he was a tall and powerfully built man in his late fifties with a smooth square face, alert blue eyes, and the almost imperceptible beginnings of a belly.

"Teel likes to b.s., you know. Once he corners you, he can go on about his rip-roaring days with the military till your head aches. So one day he gets around to telling me about his adventures during Desert Storm, how he was with the Seventy-fifth Rangers attached to the Eighty-second Airborne, did what they call direct-action missions behind enemy lines. Claims his battalion got to the Gulf in August of ninety, maybe six months before the ground war, and that he zipped back and forth over the Iraqi border blowing up Scud launchers, radar stations, that sorta thing." Silvio smiled wryly and shook his head. "Also claims that later on he fast-roped into Kuwait City and took back the U.S. embassy there."

"Sounds like an earful, all right," Bayliss said. "But how do you know for sure he isn't telling the truth? Or just maybe, uh, . . ." He groped for the right word.

"Embellishing," Munch said.

"Yeah, right."

"Let me put it this way," Silvio said, reaching into his trouser pocket for his wallet. "What I spent putting my son through the military academy is practically enough to *buy* Kuwait City. He's a full colonel now, but back in the Gulf he was a lieutenant colonel directly under Stormin' Norman himself. And unlike Teel I got *proof.*"

He opened the wallet, flipped through the plastic photo windows until he came to the picture he wanted to show the detectives, and held out the wallet.

The photograph showed a half dozen soldiers in sand camo uniforms standing beside a Humvee that was parked against a desert background, with a smiling General Norman M. Schwartzkopf posed in the center of the group.

"This one's my Steven." Silvio proudly pointed to the young man on the general's immediate right. "Amazing thing for a father to see, isn't it?"

"I'm sure it is," Munch said, hoping he sounded appropriately impressed.

"Anyway, getting back to that blowhard Teel," Silvio said, putting away his wallet, "I think it's real interesting how he was with that battalion of the Seventy-fifth, seeing as how my son told me there was only a single *company* of Rangers in the Gulf, and that it was the Fifth Special Forces Group did most of the runs into hostile territory. Also, it was teams from the Third Special Forces group with some of the Tenth that roped down into the embassy from those choppers." He shook his head again. "I'll spare you the stories about his days as a government assassin. Guess he thought I'd swallow 'em just because he carries around that James Bond piece."

"Whoa, wait a second," Munch said. "What do you mean 'James Bond piece'?"

"A Walther PPK," Silvio said. "That's the gun they always had Double-oh-seven use in the movies, but it wouldn't have done him any good in those heavy shootouts he'd get into. Too small. You wanna take somebody out with that, you'd have to get up close."

Munch was looking at him.

"Explain something to me," he said. "You're an ex-cop, right? And you had a ton of dirt on Teel right here in your office. So why in the world have you been holding out on us?"

Silvio stared back at him a moment, his eyes steady, then motioned his head around slowly to indicate the room in which they were standing.

"The paper said a homeless man killed Donna," he said. "And I like having this job."

Munch raised his eyebrows. There was plenty he felt like saying, but the main thing on his mind right now was figuring out the connection between Teel's tall tales and Seth Wilkins's yarn-spinning, and then determining what it had to do with Donna MacIntyre's murder.

He turned to Bayliss.

"I think I'd better make a call or two, then get in touch with Frank," he said, reaching into his coat for his cell phone. "I have a feeling he'll want to know about all this."

"Hello, Teel Financial Analysis."

"Mr. Teel, please."

"He's not in his office right now, may I take a message?"

"This is Detective John Munch. When's he expected back?"

"I'm afraid he's left for the afternoon, and will be out of town for at least a week."

"Out of *town?*"

"Yes, Detective."

"Ma'am, it's urgent that I reach him."

"As I said, you can leave a message. He calls in regularly to check th—"

"Reach him directly, I mean. Before he goes anywhere."

"I'm sorry, but the best I can do is try to contact him at home. His flight isn't for several hours yet—"

"I'd rather call him myself. I'll need his phone number and address, please."

"I really can't give them out—"

"This is a police matter, ma'am."

"I understand, but—"

"If you don't provide the information I can get it from the telephone company, though I'd honestly prefer not having to take the long way around."

"I realize that, too. Still—"

"Ma'am, it'd be easier for everybody if you cooperate. There's no reason for me to tell him we've even spoken, if you know what I mean."

"Well, this is quite unusual, but I suppose. . . ."

"Just a sec, let me get out my pen."

"Are you ready, Detective?"

"One more second. . . . Okay, shoot."

"The number is . . ."

"Frank?"

"Right."

"This is Munch."

"Right, what's up?"

"We're still here at Château Durham, and I think we've got enough to apply for a warrant."

"A warrant for *what?*"

"Oh, sorry, I got excited. For the search of Teel's premises."

"Talk to me."

"Well, for starters, there are threatening letters that he wrote to Donna—"

"You actually have them in your possession?"

"A whole envelope full, the most recent of them written last week. We're talking *warped.*"

"What else?"

"You wearing your hat?"

"Yeah, why?"

"Hold on to it, Frank. The head of security heard him brag about owning a Walther PPK."

"You're kidding."

"What's more, it turns out Teel's some kind of military buff. The type that attends gun conventions and swaps invented war tales with other bogus heroes. Claims to have been a special op, but it all looks like bullshit from here."

"Did the security man tell you that, too?"

"Yeah. Well, actually, Durham was the first person to clue us in about his supposed army career. The guard's the one who pegged him as a phony, though."

"What's the connection between Teel and Wilkins, do you think? I mean, both of them playing soldier?"

"Timmy and I have been batting that around ourselves. It's tough to figure."

"Agreed, but I don't believe it's any coincidence."

"Me neither. Where are you now, by the way?"

"I was just leaving the St. Ignatius soup kitchen. Wilkins's story about having eaten here the night of the killing checks out. Problem is, nobody remembers exactly when he came or left, so it doesn't amount to an alibi."

"That's too bad."

"Yeah. And I want to be careful about pushing things too far with Teel until we know more. But I agree we've got what it takes for a limited search."

"Great. Me and Timmy are gonna head over to the court and see if we can grab a judge—"

"Why don't I do that? I'm a lot closer. You know Teel's whereabouts right now?"

"According to his secretary he's on his way home. I got his address and phone number, but thought I'd touch base with you before calling him there."

"Okay, let me have the information."

"You sure you don't mind going to the courthouse?"

"No."

"All right. Actually, that'd be a big help. Gives Tim and me a chance to stop back at the Whittier Hotel.

180

There are a couple of employees we didn't get a chance to see this morning—"

"Fill me in later. I want to get going."

"Where should the three of us meet?"

"In front of Teel's building, if you ever tell me the *address*."

"Okay, sounds good, here it is. . . ."

When he was finished talking to Pembleton, Munch returned his flip phone to his coat pocket and leaned his head out the door of Walter Silvio's office.

The security man was standing at a water cooler down the hall.

"You can have your office back. Thanks for giving us some privacy," Munch called to him, and held up the envelope containing Teel's letters. "I'll have to take these."

Silvio gave him a wave of acknowledgment and kept filling his Dixie cup.

"Did I just hear you tell Frank we're heading back to the Whittier?" Bayliss asked.

"Yeah."

"Last I noticed, it was still raining out."

"Thanks, Timmy," Munch said, buttoning his coat. "You make the Weather Channel irrelevant."

As things turned out, Chris, the late-shift doorman at the Whittier Hotel, had called in sick, no doubt with rain-itis—but the coat check girl, whose name was Cathy, had arrived at work moments before Munch and Bayliss stepped in out of the tempest, and was shucking her shiny black slicker when they found her, where else, in the coat room.

"You remember a party of maybe fifteen the other night . . . bunch of Japanese businessmen, one white guy?" Bayliss asked, looking at her over the counter.

"Yes, I do, as a matter of fact," she said. "Who'd you say you are again?"

"Detective Bayliss, Baltimore City Homicide. This is my partner John M—"

"How come you want to know about Richard Teel's group?"

Bayliss looked at her. "You always know the names of the guests?"

"Well, Mr. Teel's very nice, not to mention rich and hunky," she said. "He isn't some kind of foreign spy, is he?"

"No."

"Because that's what I always thought he might be. On account of how he's with those Oriental guys a lot of the time. Plus he's so, you know, sophisticated."

"Ma'am—"

"Who am I, my mother all of a sudden?" she said. "Let's keep it Cathy, please. At least till I'm forty."

"Cathy," Bayliss said. "When the group came to pick up their coats—by the way, this was at seven-thirty, right?"

"About that, I guess," she said. "I try not to look at my watch while I'm here. Makes the time crawl."

"But you *do* remember them picking up their coats. . . ?"

"I already said so, didn't I?" she said.

"Well, not exactly. You said you remembered the group *being* here, which isn't necessarily the same thing as—"

"I *remember,* okay? That covers taking their coats when they came in, giving them back their coats when they left, and getting Mr. Teel's gym bag for him in between."

"Hold it," Bayliss said. "What's this about a gym bag?"

"You use them when you're working out at a—"

"I know what it *is,*" Bayliss said. "I asked what *about* it?"

"Oh." She shrugged. "There really isn't much to say. Mr. Teel handed it to me with his coat, came back for it maybe an hour later—"

"An hour after he arrived with the Japanese guys, you mean?" Bayliss asked.

"More or less," she said.

Which would make it somewhere around 6:15 or 6:30, he thought. Right around the time Teel's guests were sitting down to his video presentation.

"Did Teel bring the bag upstairs once you gave it to him?" he asked.

"No, I think maybe he went out to his car or something."

The detectives were looking at her.

"You think or you're sure?" Munch said.

"I *know* he left the hotel for a while, I saw him take one of the side exits. But it's not as if I would've asked where he was going," she said. "Now ask me what shade of blue his eyes are, *that* I can tell you."

183

"What makes you believe he went to his car?"

"Well, I say so because he didn't want his coat. If he'd been going anyplace far he would've worn it. That was the night the rain started, remember?"

"Yeah," Bayliss said.

"It was pretty cold outside, too," she said.

"Was he gone a while?" Bayliss asked.

"Not too long. Which is another reason I figured he just went out to a car."

"How long is 'not too long'?" Munch asked.

She sighed, as if all this fuss about time was beyond her.

"I guess it was twenty minutes or so," she said.

Which meant that, depending on when he actually left the hotel, he would have returned anywhere between 6:30 and 6:50, Bayliss thought.

Twenty minutes.

Time enough to get to Howard Street, which was a ten-minute walk at most, blow Donna Anne MacIntyre into the next world, and rush back to the conference room while his little show was still in progress.

"When he came back," Munch said, "did he still have the gym bag with him?"

A nod.

"And he checked it with you again?"

Another nod.

"And went back in the conference room?"

A third nod.

"You notice anything unusual about how he was acting at that point?"

"No," she said, giving the cops an inquisitive glance. "Jesus, he *is* a spy, isn't he?"

The detectives looked at Cathy the coat check girl without answering, both suddenly preoccupied with a very different question:

What had Teel been carrying in that gym bag?

It could have been perfect between them.

He had loved her, all he had ever done was love her, and maybe that was his downfall. Maybe his passion had been too consuming, and he had given her more of himself than she was able to give in return. Maybe . . .

Maybe . . .

Maybe he had simply loved her too much.

But it could have been so perfect.

She was the most dynamic woman he had met in his life, brilliant and strong, with that purposeful, long-legged walk of hers, that assured way of carrying herself, so aware of her body, of how good it looked in the clothes she wore, how it looked when she *moved* . . . she had been everything he'd wanted.

Everything.

He had realized this from the beginning, being with her every day, listening to her voice, seeing that brightness in her eyes. Being so close, wanting so much to touch her, and then finally asking her to dinner that night after they'd stayed late at her office . . .

It was hard to believe this was only two months ago,

back in August, when they were working the wrinkles out of their plans for the foreign trade operation.

Just last August . . .

The moment she said yes, both of them had known they were going to let it happen that night, known they wanted the same thing. August, ah God, he could still remember his expectant feeling when their eyes made contact, as if there were a hot electric wire running through his entire body. Neither of them was naive enough to have been unaware an involvement would have certain risks, but it had seemed very easy to think they could manage it, to feel confident they were experienced enough to handle any problems that might develop from mixing business with pleasure.

They made love that same night. She had initiated it, had hailed the cab after they left the restaurant and asked him if he wanted to come back to her apartment with her. Had practically undressed him in the backseat of the cab, her hand on his leg, moving up his leg to his belt, unbuckling his belt and opening his zipper and slipping her hand down the front of his pants right there in the backseat of the cab. Then, at her apartment, they had barely gotten through the door before she was all over him, almost tearing off his clothes, her eyes getting that wild, magnificent look they could have—a heightened version of what he'd glimpsed in them at her office, of what she somehow contained at the office—her eyes slitted and fiery and *needing* as his hands went up her skirt, him aching for her, her so wet underneath, their bodies grinding together, their garments scattering everywhere, his jacket, her stockings, his tie, her blouse, her panties, everywhere, leaving a trail through her apartment that ended before they reached her bed. The two of them never making it there, pulling each other down to the floor, unable to wait, rolling and moaning on the floor outside her bedroom. . . .

Even that first time, however, there had been a fracture between them, an incident that showed her to be moody and changeable . . . and that should have warned him she was a woman who would never stop pushing, no matter what you did to please her.

Lying naked with her in the dark, her back to his chest, her body pressed against him under the sheets, he'd awakened from an aqueous doze and wanted to make love again, and though she'd seemed to be asleep he had moved his hand over her, touched her breasts, touched her belly, touched her between her legs, and then, feeling she was ready, had spread her legs from behind with his knee, started to put himself inside her from behind. And suddenly she'd told him to wait, to slow down, and had squirmed away from him, telling him he was hurting her. . . .

He'd felt she was only playing. That she wanted him to take the aggressive role after having assumed it herself earlier. Wanted it a little rough. He had thought she was playing hard to get and had clamped his arm around her, pulled her closer to him under the blankets. And then she'd told him to stop, had driven her fingers into his arm and told him to stop, but he'd been so sure she really wanted it, and had rolled on top of her, pressing her belly to the mattress, spreading her legs with his knee, forcing apart her thighs. . . .

He still believed her resistance was a game. To this day, he still believed it. Only it had been *her* secret game, her way of showing the power she had simply by virtue of being a woman. He could remember the unmanning panic he had felt when his orgasm rushed over him before he was able to enter her, remember his embarrassment and anger as his semen had exploded over her buttocks, remember being disgusted by the muffled, whimpering sounds she had made into her pillow afterward, forcing tears out of herself, as if he'd really done something terrible enough to make her cry.

He had followed her when she got up to go into the living room, apologizing though he hadn't felt he had anything to be sorry about. Telling her it was a misunderstanding, although he understood all too well what had happened between them. Still, she had asked him to leave in the dead of night, put him out of her house as if he were a pet that had misbehaved.

He had made a mistake, yes, but not the one she wanted him to believe he'd made. He had thought she was different from other women, thought she was above the manipulations and challenges, the petty gender games he had come to expect . . . and he'd been wrong.

He hadn't hurt her. Had done nothing more than pick up on signals she was clearly giving off, nothing more than give her what she was asking for.

What she'd done hadn't made him need her less, though.

It had simply taught him to be careful of losing control.

He'd been unable to sleep when he got home, and had phoned her at the office the next morning, once again expressing regret over his thoughtless behavior. Saying that he'd misread her, and knew he'd done a terrible thing, and that it would never happen again. Insisting that he held her in higher regard than any woman he'd ever been with, but guessed his history of bad love affairs—affairs he implied had left him with raw emotional wounds—had somehow made him clumsy and confused when it came to physical intimacies. Adding that he knew he was fully deserving of her scorn, and wouldn't blame her if she didn't care to see him anymore, but was begging her forgiveness anyway. They got along so well, were so perfectly suited to one another, why throw away their chance at happiness over the kind of growing pains people experienced in even the best relationships? After all they had accomplished together in the workplace, he knew they could lick this problem, and that there was no limit to their potential as a couple.

Although she was icy toward him at first, he'd been able to tell she was softening by the end of the conversation. After they got off the phone, he'd sent her flowers—no common roses, but a bouquet of expensive Hawaiian orchids. Contrition with a romantic flair.

She had called to thank him that evening, and to say she looked forward to seeing him at the office the next day for a previously scheduled business meeting, cautioning him that she had come to no decision about their personal affairs.

Of course, he knew that last part wasn't true.

Two days later he had fucked her into whimpering ecstacy right in her third-floor office at Durham.

Right there in her office, where anybody could have heard them.

It had felt incredible.

Felt . . . like winning.

Things had gone well between them for several weeks after that. In bed he was intentionally restrained, and while their sex had lacked the variations he normally enjoyed, she had been an enthusiastic lover, and he was convinced she would eventually do the things he liked. The key was to be patient, and wait for the right opportunity to introduce her to them.

Labor Day weekend in the Alleghenies had seemed to be just that. He had suggested the trip and booked the lodge in which they stayed, having been there with past lovers . . . something he naturally kept to himself. In that relaxed setting, where neither of them might expect to look over their shoulders and see anyone they knew, he had thought she would be receptive to experimentation. Nothing too ambitious from his standpoint, nothing that would give her an excuse to act the way she had that first night. . . .

Of all his sexual articles he'd brought only his leather restraining cuffs.

The beginning of the holiday weekend had gone fine. On Friday they'd bicycled along the pine-flanked trails in the soaring peaks at the western edge of the state, eaten dinner at a quaint little restaurant operated by a local Indian tribe, and made love all night and late into the next morning. Still, he hadn't suggested they try anything remotely adventurous, waiting until they both had unwound after a couple of days of fresh mountain air and exercise. That night, Saturday night, they took a long walk through the woods, then went back inside, opened a bottle of expensive champagne, and started a log burning in the fireplace.

It had felt so right, so perfect . . . and would have been if she hadn't started playing games again.

Started prodding him with her questions.

He had told her about his experiences with the Rangers, just as he had told many others. The embassy rescue in Kuwait City, the covert strikes at Iraqi weapons and communications networks, commando missions in Panama during Operation Just Cause. The stories were fabrications, of course. He had never served with the Army, nor with any branch of the military. He was his own man, a leader, and only followers made good soldiers. But he was as physically capable of doing the job as someone half his age. He had made a serious hobby of learning to use firearms. He was a self-taught expert on military strategy and tactics, and could probably give seasoned combat generals tips on the latest weapons technologies. He had enough discipline for an entire squad of Rangers.

Tell that to most people, though, and what would they say? With their small minds and jealousies, they would be comparing him to the beer-bellied militiamen who ran around Oklahoma hillsides with paintball guns in their hands and copies of *Soldier of Fortune* rolled up in their back pockets. The best way to avoid that kind of insulting skepticism was to feed them the truth wrapped in an easily swallowed lie. And what harm did it do? He knew who he was. He was comfortable with himself. A certificate of honorable discharge wouldn't have made any difference.

But that second night in the Alleghenies she had needled him. Interrogated him with endless questions. Acting as if she were simply being curious.

He had known better, though. Known she was pushing him again, pushing to see how much he could take, pushing to see if his desire, and yes, his love for her—and he *had* loved her, there was no doubt about that—had made him weak.

Pushing.

It had been as if she were shining a hot, bright light in his face.

As if she didn't have a shred of trust in him.

As if she were calling him a pretender.

He didn't remember hitting her, or getting her in a body hold, or putting the leather restraints on her wrists, or what she would call the forced sex, or any of it. Everything had dissolved into a red mist and when the mist had cleared she was slumped at the foot of the bed, sobbing, her face bleeding and swollen. Her clothes had been torn, her panties pulled down around her ankles, and he knew he'd gone further than he should have . . . but was sure she must have been asking for it again. It was her fault.

Her fault he had lost control.

She'd wanted to leave after that, and had asked him to drive her someplace where she could buy a bus or railway ticket into the city. And while he'd resented her unwillingness to share the blame for the way things had turned out, that resentment had also been mingled with genuine regret this time, and he'd insisted on driving her home in his Land Rover.

He hadn't meant to go as far as he had. Hadn't meant to harm her. . . .

Everything was supposed to have been so perfect.

They left the mountains that same night. Throughout the entire ride back to Baltimore she sat solemnly beside him without saying a word, staring out the passenger window as the road spooled out behind them and the mile markers flickered by in the glow of his headlights. And with every moment that passed his sense of inevitability had grown more overwhelming. More deadening. He had realized she was going to try to end it with him, she would want out, and that this time he very likely wouldn't be able to hold on to her.

Thinking it advisable to give her a chance to cool down, he didn't make any attempt to talk things over when he dropped her off, and had only suggested that she wasn't hurt as badly as it appeared, that she'd feel a great deal better after a hot bath and a good night's sleep, and that he was sorry for letting his temper get the better of him. She had listened in inscrutable silence as he spoke, waiting for him to finish. And then she had stepped out of the car with her suitcase and walked away.

After that she had broken off all communication with him, returned none of the messages he left on her telephone answering machine, taken none of his calls at work. If it did happen that she answered the phone at home and heard his voice, she quickly hung up. On one occasion he dialed her number and got someone who introduced herself as her sister Jessica. He'd simply clicked off without leaving his name—there was no reason to talk to a member of her family, who would have heard a one-sided version of what happened, and would certainly be hostile to him.

If she had only heard him out, just once, he might have been able to carry their relationship through its crisis. Even if he hadn't succeeded, there would have been comfort knowing she'd felt it important at least to consider giving it a last shot. But she kept avoiding him.

Not wishing to cause a scene, he tried to stay away from her office, and had instead waited for her outside the condominium where she lived, but she had brushed past him as if he weren't there. Finally, he had gone to the Durham building out of desperation, walked right through her door, hoping that he could at least salvage their business association, and in that way stay close to her, and perhaps gradually win her back. That day, however, she'd threatened to call security unless he left, and said that she intended to go to the police if he kept following her—*stalking* her, as she'd put it.

As if he were a common criminal.

As if she hadn't secretly liked taking it the way he'd given it to her. . . .

For weeks afterward he couldn't sleep, and would lay awake all night thinking about her dating other men, being with other men. He knew it wouldn't be long before that happened. She was a passionate woman, and that passion would need an outlet. She would soon be fucking other men, and that was more than he could stand. He had told her so in his letters and given her a choice . . . making it clear that whatever was to be was in her hands.

He couldn't let anyone else have her.

The idea of disguising himself had really been inspired by seeing that homeless derelict on the street near her house and, ironically, hearing him jabber about being a war veteran when he'd come over to beg some spare change. Grateful, Teel had slapped a five-dollar bill into his hand. As a kind of payment.

What began as a theoretical exercise soon became a workable plan. The man was obviously a lunatic and, judging by the way he carried on in the street, probably bordered on violent psychosis. And his claims of military service had been viscerally repulsive. He was a worthless entity who bred nothing but contempt and deserved to be made a scapegoat. Furthermore, nobody would look at his face too closely. When someone like him started coming in your direction, you turned the other way. Which, in a pragmatic sense, had made him easy to impersonate, hadn't it?

The army coat he'd bought at a Goodwill store, and the wig and false beard at a place that sold theatrical supplies. He'd already owned the knit cap. And the pistol, of course. After that, it had only been a matter of watching the derelict to see if there was any pattern to his occasional absences from the block . . . tailing him to that soup kitchen and determining which nights it was open . . . and then deciding when to take the next step.

When to kill her.

The night of the reception, last Tuesday night, couldn't have been more ideal, giving him a made-to-order alibi. Timing had been critical, naturally, but he hadn't foreseen any problems. He would slip out of the room while his guests were viewing his video presentation and be back before it was over. With the lights out, and their attention focused on the screen, no one would notice him leave—and even if somebody did, it wouldn't mean anything. He would simply say he had gone to collect some important notes he had left at his office. Or something equally plausible. He was good at stories.

Once his strategy had been plotted, all he'd needed was the toughness and intelligence to methodically carry it out.

He had known he was capable of doing it.

Had known he had what it took.

He would never forget the shocked, horrified look on Donna's face the moment before he walked up and shot her in the chest, and the dawning recognition in her eyes when he'd put the gun to her forehead, and pulled the trigger those last few times to finish her. Would never forget her scream, or the sight of all that blood erupting from her shattered skull.

Would never, never forget. . . .

It was sad. So tragically sad. He had realized in a way she hadn't known what they could have accomplished together. If she'd been only half as committed as he was, only done what he told her to do, only been *true*, they could have had it all.

Now, instead, she was dead and he was leaving the country for what might be a weekend or forever. The very gym bag in which he'd carried his disguise was now packed with cash, a hundred thousand dollars in cash, an emergency fund in case he needed to stay away awhile and had any problems accessing the funds he'd stashed in that bank in the Caymans.

If not for that cop, Detective Munch, he would have stood his ground. But seeing him earlier at Durham . . . it was clear his suspicions weren't going to let up. If he hadn't already found out about the letters, he would in a matter of time. The letters, and God knew what else. Even if he never turned up any firm evidence, the scandal of an investigation would be worse than humiliating. They would dig into his background, his family life, his college records . . . uncover all the lies that were his life. In a world where perception was everything, that would be devastating. Ruinous. And he couldn't face that.

He simply could not.

It could have been perfect.

So perfect.

For both of them.

Now instead she was dead, and he was running. . . .

And damn her, damn that beautiful bitch to hell, it was all her fault.

STATE OF MARYLAND
SEARCH WARRANT AND AFFIDAVIT

<u>Frank Pembleton</u>, being sworn, says that on the basis of the information contained within this Search Warrant and Affidavit and the incorporated **Statement of Probable Cause,** he/she has probable cause to believe that the property described below is lawfully seizable pursuant to Penal Code Section 1375 as indicated below, and is now located at the locations set forth below. Wherefore, affiant requests that this Search Warrant be issued.

Frank Pembleton, NIGHT SEARCH REQUESTED YES [ ] NO [X]

(SEARCH WARRANT)

THE PEOPLE OF THE STATE OF MARYLAND TO ANY SHERIFF, POLICEMAN OR PEACE OFFICER IN THE COUNTY OF BALTIMORE: proof by affidavit having been made before me by _____Frank Pembleton_____ that there is probable cause to believe that the property described herein may be found at the locations set forth herein and that is lawfully seizable pursuant to Penal Code Section 1375 as indicated below by "x" (s) in that it:

_____ was stolen or embezzled

___X___ was used as a means of committing a felony

_____ is possessed by a person with intent to use it as a means of committing a public offense by another to whom he or she may have delivered it for the purpose of concealing it or preventing its discovery

___X___ tends to show that a felony has been committed or that a particular person has committed a felony

YOU ARE THEREFORE COMMANDED TO SEARCH:

425 Varrick Street, Baltimore, Maryland. An apartment complex located on the northwest corner of Carlson Avenue and Varrick Street. The residence is constructed of brown brick with beige stone

facing. The number is clearly painted on the door and displayed on a gray awning above the main entrance.

FOR THE FOLLOWING PROPERTY:

Traces of human blood, clothing or any material that may have been used to inflict the fatal injuries to the victim, including but not limited to a Walther PPK firearm. A dark colored knit watch cap, green army coat, gym bag and elements of a disguise used during commission of the crime. Any or all letters and paperwork indicating threats made on the life of the victim.

AND TO SEIZE IT IF FOUND: and bring it forthwith before me, or this court, at the courthouse of this court. This Search Warrant and incorporated Affidavit was sworn to and subscribed before me this ___31st___ day of ___Oct.___ , ___1997___ at ___2:45___ A.M. (P.M). Wherefore, I find probable cause for the issuance of this search Warrant and do issue it.

_Irwin Eckstein_____ , NIGHT SEARCH APPROVED YES [ ] NO [✓]
Judge of the Superior/Municipal Court, _Baltimore_____

The rain was falling in a solid curtain when the patrol car arrived at Richard Teel's residence. In the backseat, Pembleton looked out the passenger window at the main entrance. No one was going in or out of the building. No one was on the street. The only person around was the doorman, who sat behind the apartment building's double glass doors, sipping from a Styrofoam cup and browsing through a magazine on his desk.

Rain battered the awning with the same fierce, wind-driven rhythm Pembleton could hear pounding against the roof of the squad car.

He checked his watch. A little past 3:30. He had

gotten here a half hour, maybe even an hour earlier than expected. Munch and Bayliss would be surprised he'd beat them to the punch. Normally you found yourself waiting endlessly to get a warrant executed. The actual review by a judge, who determined whether it established probable cause, took only a short time. It was finding a judge to *make* the review that was enough to try anyone's patience. Give someone a magisterial robe and all of a sudden he became a leisurely fellow. Although, in fairness, some of these people had hundreds of cases on the docket every day. Not that Pembleton had ever seen a judge rush to do anything in his many years with the department.

In fact, it was only because Judge Eckstein had taken his sweet time combing his hair in the courthouse bathroom that Pembleton had been able to snag him.

Pembleton had been standing at the urinal. Eckstein had exited a stall, gone over to the sink, washed his hands, and then started to arrange his hair in such a way as to conceal the bald spot at the back of his head. Again in fairness, this wasn't easy, since the judge was also losing his hair at the front and temples of his head, making his finished appearance, which really wasn't that of a bald man at all, but of someone who had experienced some mild thinning associated with early middle age, a marvel of artful placement. . . .

At any rate, achieving that look took a while, giving Pembleton a chance to finish relieving himself, zip his fly, sidle over to the next sink over from Eckstein, and nonchalantly await the precise moment when he slipped his comb back into his trouser pocket to urge his attention.

"You're looking great, Your Honor, have you been to Florida or something?" he said, slapping the warrant application into Eckstein's palm.

The signed, stamped document was handed back to Pembleton by a court clerk less than fifteen minutes later.

To give credit where it was due, the two uniforms in the front seat of the squad car had played an equal or greater part in putting him well ahead of schedule. As he'd been leaving the courthouse, Pembleton, who knew them slightly from a previous case, had seen them exit the building just before he did and then turn toward the official parking lot. Knowing his chances of catching a bus or taxi in the middle of the storm were slim—as had Munch and Bayliss—he'd run to catch up with them and asked if they could drop him off at Varrick Street. They had not only obliged with alacrity, but had driven the entire way with their siren blaring and roof lights flashing, the racket causing traffic to part as neatly as the remaining hair on Judge Eckstein's head.

"You sure you don't want us to stick around?" the cruiser's driver asked now, glancing back over his shoulder. The name tag above his shield read Branson, like the city in Missouri where you could see the Osmonds perform minus Donny.

"Thanks, but I'll be fine," Pembleton said. "My partners ought to be here in a few minutes anyway."

"You sure?" the cop riding shotgun asked. His name

201

tag read Roswell, like the Air Force base in the Southwest where you supposedly could see little green men being dissected, also without any sign of Donny. "Hate to leave you stranded. It's raining pretty hard."

"I'd just as soon go talk to the doorman," Pembleton said. "See if he knows whether our man's around."

"Okay, you're the boss," Branson said.

Pembleton turned up the collar of his raincoat, turned down the brim of his fedora, and then started out of the car toward the building.

He had barely taken two steps across the sidewalk when he saw the doorman spring from behind his desk and open the door. At first he thought the guy might have gotten up to hold it for him, you never knew, it *was* raining outside, and he *had* gotten out of a cop car, and, Wayne Morley aside, some people in this city *did* still have respect and consideration for law officers.

Then he saw the man approaching the doors from inside the building, coming from the elevators at the rear of the lobby with one of those high, narrow suitcases you pushed along on built-in rollers. He was tall, fortyish, dark-haired, wearing a trench coat not unlike the one Pembleton had on. Carrying a gym bag over his shoulder, in addition to wheeling the suitcase. He moved without hurry into the vestibule and then spoke briefly to the doorman, who said something back to him and cocked his head toward the street.

The man with the suitcase straightened and glanced out the door, his eyes remaining on Pembleton a moment, then darting past him.

Pembleton stopped in the sheeting rain, turning to

look over his shoulder, his own eyes following the direction of the man's gaze.

Behind him, the squad car was leaving the curb, reentering traffic.

Pembleton looked back at the man with the suitcase.

Caught the man looking at him.

Their eyes met.

And held.

The man remained very still, his lips pressed together in a thin line, staring at Pembleton through the rain.

His gaze straining against Pembleton's.

The eye contact must have lasted three seconds in objective time, though it seemed to go on much longer to Pembleton. It was as if there were a high-tension wire running between them, a wire that abruptly snapped when the man turned to speak to the doorman again, then spun around on his heels, retraced his steps through the lobby, and moved toward the elevators with the wheeled suitcase in tow. The doorman scooted ahead of him to press a call button on the panel outside the elevator doors.

Pembleton stood in the rain another moment, his eyes following the man, looking at the gym bag hanging over his shoulder. Then he strode hastily under the awning and pushed through the building's entryway.

"Excuse me, sir," the doorman said, rushing back to his post to intercept him. "May I ask who you're here to visit?"

Pembleton glanced past him at the elevators. The

man with the suitcase had stepped into the same car from which he'd emerged a couple of minutes ago. With nobody else having used it, it had remained down in the lobby and opened right away.

Now the doors closed behind him and he was gone.

"The guy that was just talking to you," Pembleton said, displaying his shield and ID, "he wouldn't happen to be Richard Teel, would he?"

"Sure is." The doorman eyed his badge. "You want me to ring him for you?"

Pembleton shook his head no. He was thinking he really should have taken those two uniforms up on their offer to provide assistance. Wishing Bayliss and Munch would arrive in the next minute or so, because that was about as long as he was going to wait. These big buildings had emergency stairwells, side exits. Teel could ride the elevator up a single floor, get out, then bolt down the stairs and out of the building.

He checked the floor indicator above the elevator doors. The number 4 was lit. So was the up arrow. He stood and watched the 4 blink off and the 5 blink on. The arrow remained lit. Pembleton took a deep breath. So far, at least, it didn't seem that Teel was planning to slip out of the building.

"What apartment does Teel live in?" he asked.

"Seven-F," the doorman said. "That'd be the seventh flo—"

Pembleton was already edging past him. He sprinted to the elevators and jabbed a button with his finger.

"He tell you anything about where he was going

with those bags?" he asked, looking back at the doorman's mystified face.

"No," the doorman said. "Just asked me to hail a cab. Said he might be away on business a few weeks, wanted me to hold his mail for him."

"What happened?"

"Huh?"

"Why'd he turn around and go upstairs?"

"Don't ask me," the doorman said. "All of a sudden he sees the police car, asks how long it's been outside. Before I can answer he says to forget the taxi and does an about-face."

Pembleton stood looking at the numbers above the elevator. The up arrow had gone off but the 7 was still glowing faintly, which meant Teel's car had stopped on his floor. And was being held there. Probably he'd shoved something in the door to keep it from closing.

Pembleton shifted his eyes to the numbers over the two other elevators. Both were descending toward the lobby. One was on the fourth floor, the other on the third. *Come on, come on.* He considered using the stairs instead, but didn't like the idea of running up seven flights. It would take too long. And leave him winded. On the other hand, Teel could be waiting for him in the seventh-floor corridor outside the elevators. Waiting for the door to open so he could point a gun into the car. Hello officer, bang, bang.

He wished again that he had backup.

"Mr. Teel in some kind of trouble?" the doorman was asking.

"Nothing you need to worry about," Pembleton

said. "But I don't want you letting him know I'm on the way up. Understand?"

"Well, what if he calls down to me and asks—"

"You say I left. And another thing. I'm expecting a couple of other detectives. They're the only people I want you to let upstairs. No tenants, no visitors, no delivery boys. You have a key to stop the elevators?"

"Yeah, but—"

"I want mine to be the only one running. Cut off power to the rest."

Pembleton noticed a car had arrived on his right.

"Nobody goes up but who I told you," he said, and lunged into the waiting elevator.

He pressed the button and it started upward.

His heart pounding rapidly, his mouth filled with the metallic taste of adrenaline, Pembleton unholstered his service pistol and snapped a round into the chamber. He bent his head back and stared at the indicator lights inside the car. He had climbed to the fourth floor. Time now seemed to be rocketing along, as if compensating for its slowness when he'd faced Teel downstairs. The fifth floor flashed by much too fast. His fingers moist around the handle of the gun, he waited for the doors to open.

At the sixth floor, the elevator halted with a mild jolt.

Pembleton was out in the carpeted hallway before the doors had completely slid back on their tracks. He had pressed 6 instead of 7, thinking ahead, wanting to avoid making a cornered target of himself. Figuring Teel wouldn't expect him to take the stairs up the rest of the way.

He looked in one direction, then the other. Saw the emergency door on his right, at the end of the long, straight corridor. Hugging the wall, he rushed toward it, holding his service pistol straight down against his leg. Police style. The way it had been held by Donna Anne MacIntyre's fleeing killer, he thought.

The stairs were concrete. Fireproof. The sound of his footsteps was oddly flat and unechoing. His pulse racing, he strode up them two at a time, reached the seventh-floor landing, raised his gun in his right hand, twisted the doorknob with his left, and shouldered open the metal door.

Pembleton had just long enough to catch a glimpse of Teel standing in the empty corridor with his gun outthrust before the shot crashed from its muzzle. Small, hard bits of plaster and lathe flew from the wall to his right and showered over his hat and coat. His hand still on the doorknob, he ducked backward onto the stairwell landing, slamming the door shut, putting it between himself and Teel. There was a panel of wired glass in the door and he snatched a hurried look through it, then flattened himself against the wall as Teel squeezed his trigger again, *WHOOM,* the explosion thundering out there in the hall, the bullet slamming into the door, actually blowing a fist-sized hole in the door. This was no small-caliber assassin's gun like the one he'd used on Donna MacIntyre; this looked and sounded like a Colt .45 semiauto, a military model.

Another shot blasted through the door, the impact causing a large section of it to buckle inward. Metal splinters hailed into the landing like tiny darts, tacking against the wall and stairs. Pembleton felt a biting pain in his arm, winced, instantly looked himself over. His coat sleeve was torn below the elbow and he could see blood seeping up through the shreds of fabric. Bullet wound? No. Nothing so grave, thankfully. A fragment of the shattered slug, then. Or the door.

Still, it hurt like hell, and seemed a deep enough cut. Pembleton felt a thrill of fear and struggled to control it. He thought if he just stood where he was, Teel would keep shooting until he emptied his whole damn clip, and, God only knew, he might have spares. Probably did. He couldn't keep hugging the wall. Nor could he risk running down the stairs and inviting Teel to shoot him in the back. Bad situation. Very bad. And things weren't getting any better. So what then?

Suddenly he knew. It would be tricky, but he didn't see any choice. From what Munch had told him on the phone, Teel had been close to the brink for a long time. And had clearly gone over it when he shot and killed Donna Anne MacIntyre. He wasn't going to quit on his own.

Without giving himself a chance for second thoughts, Pembleton launched off the wall, crouched low in the middle of the landing, and fired a volley of shots directly at the door, shooting right through it. In the confined space of the stairwell the bangs sounded like grenade explosions. The door crunched out around the spots where his bullets ripped through it. Its upper hinge rattled loosely. There was a loud scream in the corridor.

His hand trembling around his gun butt, Pembleton grasped the doorknob, flung open the door, and sprang into the corridor, once again assuming a shooter's stance.

His finger on the trigger, ready to fire.

There wasn't any need for it.

Teel was curled in a fetal position on the floor, blood spurting from his right kneecap, his gun held loosely in his fingers. Pembleton rushed up through the hall and kicked the gun out of his grasp, pointing his own weapon down at him, keeping him covered.

"You're under arrest for the murder of Donna Anne MacIntyre," he said.

Teel looked up, trembling and crying, high, choked sobs coming from deep inside him in convulsive little spasms.

"Who do you think you are?" he said, his voice breaking around the words. *"Who do you fucking think you are?"*

Pembleton leaned over and handcuffed him, assuming that was a good enough answer.

NINE

BALTIMORE.

Early November.

The rain had stopped just as some people had begun to seriously consider building an ark, but the clouds were sticking around to keep them from thinking too many wicked thoughts. Or maybe so the African guys that sold umbrellas on the street could stay in business. Either way, everybody in town had continued to wear their raincoats, expecting the sky to open up at any second.

The squad room of the BCPD homicide division was depressingly dark this morning.

" 'Though seated in a wheelchair as a result of the bullet wound inflicted during his arrest, and in visible discomfort, Richard Teel has lost none of the personal appeal that made him a model of the stock market elite,' " Munch was reading aloud from the newspaper. " 'Wearing a dark Savile Row suit, he seemed relaxed declaring his innocence before the judge, waving and smiling at courtroom observers and members of the press—'"

"Last night a legal commentator on TV called him a stud-muffin," Pembleton said.

Munch looked at him over the top of his paper.

"I kid you not," Pembleton said, making the scout's honor sign. "She's a defense lawyer, though, so it stands to reason."

"Speaking of which, you hear who Teel got to represent him?" Kellerman said from his desk.

Pembleton nodded. For the last couple of weeks, Teel had been assembling a team of million-dollar attorneys to outscheme all others before it, headed up by a porcine Florida loudmouth who—oh, wonderment— had once been a member of the bunch that helped free the celebrity killer out in L.A. Teel had also hired a large New York public relations firm to spin out daily press releases for him, and was said to be launching an Internet site to further spread his gospel. Although the Teel defense strategy remained officially undisclosed, there already had been leaks suggesting it would be a complicated approach involving evidence contamination, improper police conduct, and claims that Teel was suffering from some sort of executive stress disorder. The way things were going, Pembleton figured he'd probably be the guy behind bars before it was all over.

"'And the seasons, they go round and round,'" he muttered. "You ask me, Teel will—"

There was a sudden, loud clatter from over where

Bayliss sat, and Pembleton turned to see what was going on, raising his eyebrows in confusion.

Bayliss had pulled the top drawer out of his desk and turned it upside down over his trash can. Playing cards, some loose, some in unopened packs, were tumbling into the garbage along with linking metal rings, lengths of cut rope, trick boxes, brightly colored silk handkerchiefs, spools of crepe paper ribbon, variously sized balls and cups, a Chinese fan, dummy eggs, a black wand, and finally, his 1910 magician's handbook, which went out in a flutter of lopped and yellowed pages.

"Control, *shit!*" Bayliss hollered.

Pembleton and the others sat there in silence for almost five minutes, alternately watching him and trading puzzled glances and shrugs.

When he was finished emptying the props and accessories from the drawer, Bayliss set it back on its tracks above the kneehole of his desk, slammed it shut, then lowered himself into his chair, looking down at the floor.

"Great trick," Munch said. "Care to tell us what it was all about?"

After a long while Bayliss looked up, and whatever Munch saw in his clear blue eyes made him feel something very close to shock.

"Believe me," he said. "You never want to know."